Book One of The Defra Elf Saga

Blood Oath Trials

Jordan Nuttall

Plexus Publications

Published by Plexus Publications LLC

www.plexuspublications.com

Edited by Jana Spivey Enderle

Cover Illustrated by Cody Robles

ISBN: 9780997669022

Acknowledgements

I have to thank my Dad and Mom for all of their help in my writing process. Without them everything would have been much harder. A special thanks to my good friends who listened to my ideas and read my story, especially LJ, Ben, and Jason. I am very grateful for my talented editor Jana and my illustrator Cody. A big thank you to Matt for helping me get this published and out there for others to read. There are many more that should be thanked, but I do not wish to write a novel of thank-yous so to all those who have helped me over the years, thank you.

Introduction

Looking down upon his son filled his heart with pride, momentarily causing the short brown strands of his hair to turn darker. It made the brown stand out in stark contrast among the other four colors of his hair. He looked over to his wife; her long multicolored hair was beautiful. Unlike his, which was shaved short, her hair flowed midway down her back. Beauty was not the only thought to come to his mind when he beheld the five colors of his wife's hair. Power came to his mind as well, as each color represented a unique magical ability. Thinking of those colors and the significance of their power caused him to reflect upon his union to her. It had been a prearranged one. Everyone within the village knew it was going to happen. They were the only two who together could make the long sought-after Chromatic Defra Elf a reality.

His village had been trying to create a Defra which possessed all the colors of magic long before he was born. The effort dated all the way back to the end of the Great Civil War, which split the Defra Elves into two villages. Each village had one of the original powers at their head. One side was led by the Defra with the powers of death. The other side was led by the Defra with the powers of life. His village, the Life Defra village, believed a combination of all the minor colors would lead to the eventual downfall of the Death Defra village. Now, after so many years, his son had the hopes of being the long-awaited Chromatic.

Looking back down at his son, whose hair was currently green, he said, “Elia, he could be it. He could be what we’ve all been waiting for.” He was trying not to get too excited, but he couldn't help it. They had six kids before this one. Their third child had been the closest, exhibiting seven of the ten powers. The three afterward had four or less. They'd begun to give up hope. This son was already up to six colors on the first day.

“Yes, I know, Zygan. I’ve been thinking the same thing,” Elia replied, reaching out to grasp his hand before continuing, “What will happen if he is?” He could feel her hands trembling. He knew her fear was for the child's potential life of endless training in solitude.

“He will, no doubt, be taken to be trained by the masters in order to lead us against the Black Defra.” He squeezed her hand to try to reassure her it would be okay anyway.

“I hope we will be able to raise him beneath our care. I don’t want to have a room full of elite Defra Elves do it,” Elia said with a few tears running down her cheeks, which made her orange strands of hair fade to a lighter shade. Her love for each of their children ran deep. Zygan honestly did not mind if they were unable to raise their child if it would mean the betterment of their village.

“Don’t worry, my love. I will make sure you get to care for him, like our other six children,” Zygan told her, bringing her into his arms. Elia's trembling subsided slightly. He wasn’t sure how he would manage it. He would figure it out. He knew it was what she needed to hear from him. Though their union had been arranged, he still found he loved her. He wanted only the best for her. “Let’s go to bed and see what life brings us tomorrow.”

"It feels like I need to stay here. What if something happens to him?" Elia whispered. Her heart beat faster against him as she spoke. Zygan stared past her into the dark hallway, once again marveling at her intense love for their children.

"Nothing is going to happen to him. Our room is right next to his. It'll be okay, come to bed with me." His voice was gentle. His hands caressed her shoulders lightly. Elia breathed in deeply, moving further into his arms.

"Okay," she replied reluctantly with one last glance at their son. The room was left in silence. The moon slowly rose high into the starry night sky. An eerie silence fell over the forest. It was as if the world was holding its breath, waiting to see how things would turn out.

A soft squelching noise echoed through the silence. A large, hideous creature entered the clearing from the forest surrounding the village. The noise had come from the slime oozing out of the many pores dotting his body. It created a thin layer, covering him from head to toe. Excess slime dripped to the ground behind him. His eight bright red eyes searched the surroundings for his destination. A second set of red eyes emerged behind the first. "Why is some baby so important to the Ancient Ones?" questioned the second one.

"I don't know. We do what they say to do because we know they know what is best," the first replied, sliding his large, slimy legs forward. He was unable to lift them off the ground. Their massive bodies had not been blessed with the proper joints in their legs. It made any travel a long, arduous process. He wore special gloves upon two of his four hands, so as not to harm the baby with his acidic slime. He swung the door to the appropriate house open, careful to not make any sound. The wood burned beneath his touch. He quickly found the room where the baby rested. Before entering, he glanced around to make sure no one had seen him. Once reassured his presence was still unknown, he slid to the bedside.

He picked up the small form with green hair. As he did so, the baby's hair turned blue. He immediately swung his body around to leave the room. The process was far faster than it should have been for someone his size. His agility was one of the reasons he was chosen for this task. His companion was in the hall keeping guard. He motioned for them to leave. There was no need to remind him to be quiet. They were moments away from succeeding with the most dangerous part of their mission when the baby cried out. He wasn't sure how such a loud sound came from such a small thing.

"Quick! Quiet the baby. I'll go intercept the parents," his companion declared, turning to block anyone who tried to come. He grabbed an oddly-shaped object from his bag and stuck it into the baby's mouth.

"Zygan, the baby!" came a woman's scream. They'd already decided if it came to a fight, he would be the one to leave while his companion stayed to fight. He used his back eyes to watch his friend readying himself for the encounter. His friend stayed behind, even with the knowledge of how strong the baby's parents were. They were capable of killing him. It did not matter to him; he would do whatever necessary to create enough time to ensure their success.

"It's the Groucken," said a voice close by.

The eight-foot Groucken raised his shield upward as a large spear with water and earth elements twirling around it came flying straight for him. He was a little surprised when upon impact the two elements shot out sideways. They came toward his friend from both sides. The water formed itself into a spike of ice and the earth into a war hammer. He saw his friend move slightly toward the spike to smash it with his fist. His slime devoured the magic within it. Then he swung his shield around to intercept the war hammer.

His friend disappeared from view. He strained his eyes to see more. It was impossible. There were too many trees blocking his view. He could feel the battle continue to rage behind him. They were connected to each other through an emotional bond. He carried the baby as carefully as possible so as not to harm him. He knew his friend would not go down without doing some considerable damage. The creations of Bourden underestimated the tremendous power of his race. Most likely because they forgot it was from them that their origins lay. The sad thing was, they didn't even want to kill anyone. They had to make sure the Defra could not recover the child; killing was a forced necessity. What they wanted did not matter. What mattered was completing his mission.

Fifteen minutes later, he felt his friend die. His eyes turned blue for a few moments then reverted back to red. It was a unique phenomenon to his people. It rarely occurred. It only happened in times of extreme loss or pain. He'd known his friend for over ten thousand years. Many people would one day be grateful for his friend's sacrifice.

He traveled southeast silently reflecting on his friend's life until he reached the current location of the Elves in Bigor Forest. The Defra were descendants of these Elves, separated long ago. Without drawing attention to himself he moved toward the Queen's Tree. He sat the baby next to it. He pulled the object from its mouth. It started crying again the instant it was gone. With his job done he left the area. The only indication of his presence was the burnt trail he left behind. A short time later, the queen emerged from the tree she'd been sleeping in. She picked up the baby. It surprised her when it stopped crying. Her heart was touched by its innocence, so she went to seek out the king.

Once the king emerged from his own tree, she explained softly, “This baby was abandoned next to my tree with no one to care for it. I believe it is a gift from someone.”

The king looked upon the baby’s bright orange hair, noticing its eyes were a swirl of many colors, among those colors was orange. He knew it was not from their city. They had banished the Defra from their lands many centuries ago. Their existence was a royal secret. Common knowledge of it was long forgotten. He couldn't help wondering how the baby could have gotten here from its homeland. He asked his wife, “Where do you think this baby comes from?”

“Where is it from?” She replied in question. She must have been able to tell he knew the answer to his own question. She knew him too well.

The king shook his head, “It matters not. I know I have not been able to give you a child, so if it is your wish to keep this one, then I will accept.”

“It is my wish,” The queen replied gently.

“Then what shall be his name?” He asked her. He knew this decision could one day lead to problems. He would have to deal with those when they came.

“Kelovin.”

Chapter One

It was midday, the sun high above the tree line shedding what light it could through Bigor Forest. The forest was known to be the home of Elves. It had been for many centuries. If they had not been awake, however, the common eye would not have been able to tell there was a large thriving city of them right in the middle of Bigor Forest. There were neither homes nor castles; there were no visible torches or other sources of light. Only proud, red cedar trees looming over two hundred feet into the sky could be seen. In truth, it only seemed abandoned when the city slept. During the day, it was a different sight. Thousands of Elves roamed within the forest, all busily performing various tasks.

"So, why does your father want to see you, anyway?" Pelmor asked. Pelmor was a young Elf with blond hair. His eyes were dark brown. From the smile on his face, Kelovin could tell Pelmor already thought he knew the answer.

"I don't know, probably to yell at me again as usual," Kelovin shrugged his shoulders. He was the same age as Pelmor. His hair was a light shade of gold with light golden eyes. They were walking among the trees slowly while they conversed, not paying attention to their surroundings.

"Do you think he found out about Kya?" Pelmor asked.

"I don't know how he would have. Then again, my father finds out about everything I do. If it isn't that, I'm not sure what else it could be," Kelovin confessed. His father would be angry if Kelovin was being summoned about the girl. He'd already broken this particular rule several times before with other girls.

"So? You haven't been going around breaking any of the other rules you must adhere to as prince," Pelmor said. The way he said it made it less of a question and more of a surprised statement. It was true Kelovin was not one to follow the rules, but it was an unfair assessment as he saw it. The only reason he didn't was because all of the rules his father imposed upon him were ridiculous. Kelovin felt no one in their right mind could follow them all.

"No, I didn't break any of the others recently. I might be wrong. There are so damn many it's hard to keep up with them all, perhaps I forgot one. I swear, my father makes them up every day to restrict me more. My life sucks." Kelovin dropped his head, sighing as loud as he could. He hoped to get some sympathy from his friend.

"Man, I can't believe you don't like being the king's son!" Pelmor declared with his eyes getting wider. "If I were in your shoes, I would be the happiest Elf alive." Apparently, Kelovin wasn't going to get any sympathy from Pelmor today.

"If you want it, you can have it," Kelovin said, no longer interested in their conversation. He wished people would leave him alone about having responsibility simply because he was royalty. He wanted to be free to do whatever he wished.

"But why?" persisted Pelmor in his usual prodding, playful voice. He always adopted that voice when he was expressing disagreement with someone. He did it in order to pass off his views as a joke when people became angry or disagreed with him. Kelovin had long since learned he was usually serious.

"Because this kind of life isn't me. I want to go out into the world. Have an adventure, accomplish great feats, and do things most people don't even dream of doing. I want to experience all life has to offer. Not live with a boring people who feel peaceful harmony is all there is to life," Kelovin explained, despair in his voice. He knew he would never have the chance to carry out all his dreams. He wished it could be possible--every inch of him wanted it to be possible. He was dying to get out into the world outside of Reshyr.

"Don't you hear yourself? Peace is what every nation in the world looks for. We have it. How can you not be happy with peace and harmony?" Pelmor asked.

"Yes, peace is great, but I feel like I was born to travel and do great things. It is a freedom I cannot experience beneath the watchful eye of my father, not to mention every other Elf. I want to experience true freedom. I can't have freedom while here in Reshyr," Kelovin said.

"Well, I think it all sounds great when you say it, but as Elvin royalty, you have to live in reality. You have to try to forget about those crazy ideas. It is your responsibility to lead this city if your father should die. Your father makes these rules to keep you out of harm's way," Pelmor told him.

"Now you sound like my father," Kelovin sighed.

"I'm trying to help," Pelmor said, throwing his hands up in a sign of surrender.

"Yeah, well, if you want to help so bad, then pick the right side. I don't need lectures from you on top of what I get from my father already," Kelovin said. He looked up to find they had already arrived at his father's court.

At first glance, it wasn't much different than the rest of the forest. It was a group of thicker trees growing closer together than the rest. Within the clump of trees, a small path led to a small circular clearing. The trees surrounding it grew close enough together there was barely a hands-breadth between them which made it so the pathway was the only way of getting to the clearing within. Not a single branch was allowed to shade the path from above, in order to allow the sun's light to flood into it. Passing into it almost blinded him every time. It was one of the many devious tricks Elvin kings used to gain the upper hand in all situations.

Within the circle, at the end of the path, was a throne. It was made from living vines and branches from the surrounding trees. Magic aided them in forming the majestic, yet simple throne in which his father sat.

Kelovin changed his posture. He didn't need to give his father anything else to ride him about. He tried his best to compose a better attitude as he walked up toward the throne. When he was a respectable distance away Kelovin said, "You called for me father?"

"Yes, I have some things to discuss with you," he answered. His face was emotionless, his manner serious. Kelovin waited for him to proceed. So, he did. "It has come to my attention you have been romantically seeing someone. Is this true?"

"Yes, father," Kelovin replied, knowing his father would have already known. He only asked to see if Kelovin would lie. His father could be deceptive, especially when he wanted to find even more fault than he already had.

"I believe we've already discussed this before, Kelovin. I do not feel it wise for you to be doing so. You will only create jealousy among the other Elves. It will bring unnecessary contention."

"What if I want them to be envious of being with me?" Kelovin interrupted his father with a smirk. He was tired of his father trying to control his life. Yet, even while he spoke, part of him knew he should not push things too far. It would do him no good to find himself punished because of ill-spoken words.

"This is not a game, Kelovin," his father declared. His face became red while his voice got higher. His father did not show visible emotion often. "Now, I want you to discontinue seeing her. You will wait until your mother and I find a suitable companion for you."

"Father, you can't control every aspect of my life. It is not fair, I want to be like any other normal Elf of the village," Kelovin retorted. He allowed his voice to rise even louder than his father's, "When will you let me go out on my own? I want to have my own life. I can make my own decisions."

His father sat silently for a moment. It made Kelovin nervous, wondering if perhaps he had already pushed things too far. Finally, in a slightly exasperated tone, his father said, "Very well, your mother and I have been talking about it. If you want a chance to get out on your own to experience the world, then that's what you'll get. I have been trying to think of someone I can send out into the world to find us one of the ancient artifacts of the gods. Perhaps you are perfect for the task."

Kelovin stood speechless for several moments, "Are you serious?" was all he could manage to say when he found his voice.

"You will take Pelmor and Ryga with you and leave tomorrow at first light. The humans and Dwarves each have obtained one of these artifacts. We can't leave ourselves without advantage. Perhaps this experience will better help you fulfill your duties as an Elvin prince," his father replied as an answer.

"Thank you, Father," Kelovin said calmly, while on the inside he could hardly hold his joy within. "You will not be disappointed; I will find this artifact and bring it back to you."

"Yes, well, you best prepare. Ryga is already waiting for you two. You are dismissed." Kelovin nodded. He left back the way he came, but before he could make it all the way out his father added, “Kelovin, you and this girl are through now.”

“Yes, Father,” Kelovin answered promptly, trying hard not to sound excited. It was a small price to pay for being able to leave Reshyr. Once he was outside the path, Pelmor walked to his side, remaining silent. Kelovin continued to put distance between them and the clearing. When they were well out of earshot, Pelmor said, “I can’t believe your father is letting you leave.”

“I know; this is incredible. Do you realize what this means, Pelmor?” Kelovin asked putting his hand upon Pelmor's shoulder.

“Well, I have a few ideas. What are you thinking?” Pelmor replied. He knew Kelovin didn’t want to hear what he thought at the moment.

“This means we are going to be free to do whatever we want, whenever we want. We’ll be able to explore the world. We’ll be able to do things we only dreamed of doing before,” Kelovin’s joy was almost contagious enough to get anyone excited.

“Yes...with Ryga watching over us and your father expecting us to return with some mysterious artifact. Might I mention, we don’t even know where to begin looking for the thing,” Pelmor said, not as enthusiastically.

“None of it matters, my friend. We will storm the world becoming great adventurers. We’ll be new heroes for them to write legends about. We will find this artifact, thus bringing the Elvin race to equal standing with the rest of the races. Everyone will know our names. Then, you’ll be able to have any Elvin girl you want,” Kelovin exclaimed with long, sweeping hand movements. He wanted to get Pelmor as excited as he was about the whole thing.

Pelmor only looked at him as though he were crazy, “You know Kelovin, sometimes I wonder if you weren't meant to be born as an Elf. Your behavior is way different than everyone else's, not to mention your way of thinking."

Pelmor's words were almost enough to deflate the joy Kelovin felt. Being so different from all of the other Elves had always been one of the most difficult things he had to deal with in his life. When he was young, he was unable to do the things all Elvin kind was capable of. It led to him being shunned by the other kids. Everyone treated him as an outsider, except Pelmor. It was the reason why they had become such great friends. "I'm sorry I have made you feel that way, Pelmor," Kelovin said casting his eyes toward the ground.

"No, come on, Kelovin. You know I'm only playing," Pelmor exclaimed, adopting his playful voice again, "I'm definitely excited for this opportunity. We're going to be heroes!"

"Now you're getting what I'm saying," Kelovin grinned widely, accepting Pelmor's words as an apology. "We will be more than heroes. We will be legends, as the first great Elvin king is. Can you imagine?" Kelovin was never known to set his expectations low.

"Well, if we're going to be legends then I better prepare to leave," Pelmor said to indicate his departure. "There is much an Elf may need if they expect to rival Beldon the Great."

"Just be prepared for the experience of a lifetime to start tomorrow. You shall see, Pelmor. I have a great feeling about this. It will be like nothing we've ever known," Kelovin called to his friend's back. Pelmor continued on his way. Kelovin was left standing by himself with more energy than he could handle. After a moment's thought, Kelovin took off running for the other side of the village. His keen Elvin eyesight allowed him to weave a path between the trees at a far greater speed than most other humanoids.

He came out into a clearing with a large pond in the middle. They called it the Great Spring because it was the largest pond they'd ever seen fed by a natural spring. Kelovin felt they could have done better naming it, but that was not one of his major concerns at the moment. He sped south around the Great Spring to the Sleeping Trees. He was soon forced to slow to a walk, however, as he came into view of groups of Elves walking around, going about their own business. His father would not be happy if he was reported to have been running around like a child within the Sleeping Trees. He was told such things were not what royalty did. Royalty did not often visit the Sleeping Trees, so they must appear dignified when visiting. There was so much royalty did not do it made him wonder how any of them ever managed to live their entire boring lives.

The Sleeping Trees were all tall oaks reaching high into the sky. They stood out from among the surrounding red cedar trees of Bigor Forest. The change in trees was an oddity that happened long ago which Kelovin could not remember the reason for. There was always a blanket of leaves upon the floor beneath them. They felt soft under his feet. Kya's tree was not far from where he entered–several trees south and about twenty to the west. Even being so close, it had taken him a long time to memorize its location. He'd gotten lost several times when he first began visiting.

"Kelovin," came Kya's beautiful voice. She came into view seconds later. She looked as beautiful as her voice sounded. Her long, slender body moved fluidly toward him. She looked at him with accusing eyes. "I've been wondering when you would come to visit me. It has been so long."

In truth, he had seen her only yesterday. He enjoyed it when she behaved like she was unable to live without him. He did not believe she truly had those kinds of feelings, even with how convincing she made it seem. Knowing didn't stop him from enjoying it. Kelovin grinned as he told her, “Sometimes we must wait for the great things we desire in life.”

“Yes, but you have let me wait far too long.” Kya slipped a hand around his waist to draw him close to her. Rising to the tips of her toes, she planted a soft kiss upon his lips. It made his heart pump faster. Kya was the most satisfying lover Kelovin had ever had.

“I need to talk to you,” Kelovin said. He chose to remain within her embrace for a moment longer. She must not have taken him seriously because instead of listening, she went in for another kiss. This time Kelovin found himself pulling away from her. She looked up at him, her eyebrows furrowing together as though she was trying to solve some complex puzzle. He was not usually the one to pull away from intimacy.

“What is it, my prince?” She had addressed him as *her prince* ever since he met her. When they had first met, she had said it out of respect. Now, after they had been seeing each for some time, it was said in an affectionate way.

“My father has commanded me to no longer see you,” Kelovin explained. Had his father not offered the chance to leave, it was likely he would not have obeyed him. Now, he found it was easier than he could have imagined. He had never fallen in love with the girl, even if he was fond of spending time with her.

“Why?” she began, her eyes darted back and forth as she searched for an answer. “No, we don’t have to. We can run away together. They can’t keep us apart.” Her face pleaded for him to say yes. Yet, when he looked into her eyes he could see it was not true love driving her plea. She was more in love with his royalty than she was with him. He had known it for a long time already. It had never bothered him enough to quit seeing her.

Knowing her true feelings made it easier for Kelovin to say, "No, we can't, Kya. I am to leave tomorrow with Ryga and Pelmor on an important quest for the king. It is going to affect all of Elvin kind, so I must go. You will find someone else. You are wonderful, after all. When I return from my quest I am sure you will have already found your true companion."

She realized he was not going to be persuaded to change his mind because her manner changed quickly. The hurt look was replaced with a playful attitude which had been part of what originally drew him to her. She closed the gap between them once more. "We may have to split up, my prince, but we still have today together. We can make the most of it. We can spend one last day having the kind of fun your father would disapprove of."

She certainly knew how to tempt him. He raised his head, closing his eyes, to think a moment. He wanted to say yes. The fear of his father discovering his actions waded in the back of his mind, preventing him from doing so. His father had eyes and ears everywhere in the city– especially within the Sleeping Trees. In the end, the choice was simple. There was no way he could risk losing his ticket out of Reshyr. "I'm sorry, Kya, I cannot. I only came to say goodbye."

"How unfortunate. I'll never forget the time we've had together, my prince," Kya said, caressing his arm gently before walking away from him. Kelovin ripped his attention away from her receding form before he let himself change his mind. It had been risky to come say goodbye to her. Sometimes his will was not as strong as he wished it was. Leaving without saying goodbye would not have felt right. He walked back the way he came, then turned north upon reaching the Great Spring once more.

North of the Great Spring lay the only existing building within their Elvin city. It was not much of a building. There was only a fire pit made of bricks, an anvil, and a small rack of tools housed under a thin metal roof held up by four poles. To even build so little without breaking the oath Beldon had made with the trees, allowing them to sleep safely within their confines, had been difficult. His teacher, Ryga, had taught him about it as a child. It was one of the few things he'd actually paid attention to. Mostly, because he loved hearing of the great things Beldon had done. As far as he knew, Beldon was the only Elf in all of history to be adventurous. The best part was that Beldon had been a king. He always tried to bring this up with his father. His father always said it was simply a different time back then.

"Ah, young Kelovin Zyglan come to pay me a visit," a strong voice called from within the forge. "I suspect this is because you shall be leaving next sunrise and would have your sword prepared for the journey ahead."

"How did you know, Corrae?" Kelovin asked, coming close enough to see the smith. He was a small Elf, muscled far more than any he'd ever seen. His skin was drawn tight, highlighting each of the many muscles in his body.

Corrae left whatever it was he was working on to direct his attention to Kelovin. "King Brodas sent someone to inform me of it already. I have prepared your weapon as well. You'll find it is battle-ready." Kelovin was not surprised by the smith's answer. His father never did anything on the spur of the moment. Everything was always carefully calculated, then planned accordingly. Corrae extended a long sword hilt-first to him.

Kelovin took the sword. He gave it a few practice swings before looking it over. The sword was excellently made; Corrae was the one who made it, after all. Nothing he ever did turned out any less than excellent. "It is wonderful," Kelovin told him. "You truly are a great smith, Corrae."

He nodded a thank you to the compliment. "I should be. It is what I've been doing my entire life." It was no exaggeration, either. Corrae had been taught to be a smith ever since he could walk. Only one blacksmith was ever allowed within the Elvin city. In order to ensure their smith was talented, the king would choose a child from birth to be the next smith when the old one had little life left in him. "It is no Dwarven blade," Corrae added sadly.

Dwarven blades were the greatest weapons to wield. All of the great heroes of the past wielded one. The Dwarves had perfected the technique of infusing weapons with magic long ago– a feat no one else could lay claim to. His father had one such blade called Nightbringer. If the blade even scratched an enemy, it would take their sight from them. Nightbringer had been passed down from king to king for thousands of years. "Still, it is a good sword," Kelovin said continuing to swing the sword around.

"Well, now you have it, so I ought to pass along the message I was given. Ryga is looking for you. He wants you to meet him at the royal training grounds." Corrae turned back to his work, hefting his great hammer once more. Kelovin wanted to keep talking to Corrae, but it would do no good to distract him from his work, so he left instead.

He knew he probably had loads of work to get done with Ryga anyway, he always did. On his way out, he grabbed his scabbard from one of the poles. He fastened it around his waist before sheathing the new sword. To get to Ryga he had to go north of where his father sat upon the throne. The royal training grounds looked exactly the same as the rest of the forest, only with a bit more space between the trees for easier maneuvering.

"I've been waiting for you, Prince Kelovin," Ryga called. He was sitting on the ground in the middle of the training grounds. Even from a sitting position, it was easy to tell Ryga was an unusually tall Elf. Ryga had been his teacher for as long as he could remember. He was one of the only Elves he knew personally who still formally addressed him with his title.

"Corrae told me so," Kelovin replied. He approached Ryga warily. He could never be sure when Ryga would choose to teach him a lesson about always being prepared. He thought it was silly for Ryga to test him by attacking at random moments. He said as much to him every time he was caught by surprise by one such attack. Ryga would always remind him the randomness of the attacks was the point of always being prepared. He felt it was an unnecessary lesson. It never seemed likely to him that he would be attacked at random while he was safely tucked away in the heart of Reshyr.

"Come sit by me, I must speak with you about our travel together." Ryga motioned to a spot next to his. Kelovin took the indicated spot. He didn't take his eyes off his teacher for a second. When Kelovin was seated in a satisfactory position, one in which he could spring to his feet in an instant, Ryga continued, "There are some rules I need to discuss with you. You will be expected to follow them while we are away from the city."

Kelovin couldn't help sighing irritably. The thought had not occurred to him before, but Ryga was only being sent with him to be his babysitter. Having someone constantly watch over him was sure to ruin his path to greatness. How would he ever be able to become a legend if all the stories began with Ryga protecting him or treating him like a child? "Why must there be rules? Why can't we go out there and do whatever fate has in store for us?" Kelovin asked, although he already knew the answer.

"Because you are a prince. As a prince, you must be kept out of harm's way. Will the gods it does not happen for a long time, but should something happen to your father, then the kingdom would fall to you to rule. You can't rule if you are dead. So, the first rule, you must at all times obey my commands.

Secondly, you must never reveal to anyone you are an Elvin prince. Knowledge of who you are could be extremely dangerous. You never know what a person would do if they knew of your importance. Finally, you must never leave my presence."

"With rules like those, I will not be the one doing the adventuring. It will be you becoming a legend. I shall never get to do anything worth talking about," Kelovin muttered angrily. As he said it, realization came upon him. His father had never intended to send him on a real journey. He had meant only to send him out with Ryga for a walk. The mission was designed to disguise the walk as an important journey. They probably weren't expected to return with the artifact at all. Well, he would make sure to disappoint his father. He would force it to turn into the real thing. Outside Reshyr there would only be Ryga there to stop him.

"Trust me, Prince Kelovin. After we've been out there for a while you will be glad of the rules. Before we can leave, you are going to have to make the blood oath swearing you will follow my rules."

"What? No. I refuse to make the oath," Kelovin declared, rising from the ground. The blood oath was a ceremony performed between two Elves. It caused those who made it unable to break any promise they made. The powerful magic was ancient going back several generations of Elves. "How can my father expect me to agree with this? The second there is trouble, you will command me to come home. My quest will never have even started."

"I promise I will not send you home at the first sign of danger—only if I feel things beginning to get out of hand. Your father has already said we will not be going if you don't make the oath. It is King Brodas's direct command." Ryga remained seated with part of his weight leaning back on his hands behind him. He waited for Kelovin to process everything.

Kelovin paced back and forth, weighing out the options in his head. He couldn't run away to do what he wanted by himself. His father would have brought him back within a day's time. If he stayed here, his life would continue on as boring as ever except he would not have Kya to go to anymore. He stopped pacing. He looked Ryga in the eyes before saying, "Fine, I will agree to it. Something is better than nothing, but I will not pretend to be happy about it."

"I would have been surprised if you had," Ryga replied. He rose from the ground. Ryga bowed his head in concentration. The trees around them groaned. They shifted from their spots until they formed a perfect circle. Kelovin was always amazed by the simple magic. Trees are large things to be moving around so easily. He and Ryga stood in the center of the trees facing each other.

Kelovin pulled a small dagger from his boot then used it to prick his finger. He held out his hand for Ryga to take. Ryga pricked his own finger before taking it. Once their hands were joined, vines from the trees shot out to wrap around their arms. The vines covered from their fingertips up to their shoulder blades making it look as though they were connected together by a thick arm made of vines.

"Don't forget, we aren't starting this journey until tomorrow," Ryga said.

Kelovin scowled, "I know. Honestly, these things aren't hard." Within himself, he thanked Ryga for the reminder. He would never have thought of it by himself while speaking the oath.

Kelovin spoke the words of the oath first, "I, Kelovin Zyglan, make this oath by the blood of my body, binding my body and soul to the oath I shall speak. I covenant, beginning upon our departure tomorrow, I will obey all the commands given to me by

Ryga except those which conflict with my oath to the king. I will never reveal my identity as a prince except as commanded by the king. I shall never leave Ryga's presence except as commanded by the king or by Ryga."

Once he'd finished, Ryga spoke, "I seal this oath created by Kelovin by receiving his blood," the vines turned a hue of red as he spoke the words. "I declare: if this oath shall be broken, he shall feel unbearable pain until he intends to obey the oath." Ryga shut his eyes to concentrate harder as he finished the last part of the oath. The vines around their arms pulsed twice before disintegrating to dust. The trees around them returned to their normal positions.

"You did well, Prince Kelovin, even with all of the exceptions," Ryga said with a pat on his shoulder. When performing blood oaths such as the one they did, they had to be sure to work around the king's oath. The king's oath was made by every Elf of the city as soon as they were old enough to memorize the words to it. It prevented any rebellion or disobedience from ever rising among the Elves. Elvin kings were not like human ones. They did not have to worry about abuse of the oath, as the humans would have. Humans were controlled by their emotions too easily, especially when it came to greed for wealth or power.

"I've seen hundreds of them performed. It is not hard to learn." Kelovin said, his scowl deepening. He turned to stomp away, but before he could, Ryga spoke again.

"Now we are done with those preparations, we can move on to some sword practice. It will cheer you up. Draw your sword." The notion of dueling with Ryga did make him happy, but he would never admit it if he was asked. He sighed to make sure Ryga knew he was not going to be tricked into a happy mood. Kelovin drew his sword then circled around Ryga. He had fought Ryga many times before—all of them led to defeat. This time would be different. Ryga stood in the center at the ready, spinning around as Kelovin circled. He saw his opening. Ryga was a half-step slow in spinning to face him. He lunged quickly, blade pointed to kill.

Ryga dodged sideways while batting his sword away. He found himself parrying Ryga's follow-up attacks frantically. The Elf was quick and sure-footed. Kelovin planted his foot in order to swing hard. When he connected with Ryga's blade, a jolt ran through his arms nearly causing him to lose his grip. The attack succeeded in forcing Ryga backward. Kelovin readjusted himself while Ryga waited for his approach again. He did not make Ryga wait long. Kelovin came at him with an overhead swing, putting all the strength he could muster into it.

He was quick enough to force Ryga to parry rather than dodge. Kelovin smirked triumphantly as Ryga lost balance against the force, falling backward. He went in to finish the fight. His triumph was cut short when the world tilted; his legs were swept out from beneath him. Ryga was back to his feet far faster than should have been possible. Kelovin was still on his knees when the attacks came. It was only seconds before Ryga gained the upper hand, holding the point of his sword against Kelovin's chest.

"Your strength is amazing. You must know, strength alone is not able to win all your fights. You must refine your technique. Always remember those who attack second almost always win the advantage," Ryga tutored him.

Ryga's words only made Kelovin angrier about losing. "Again," Kelovin demanded through clenched teeth. They dueled long into the evening. Ryga caused the vines to glow to provide them with light after the sun sank below the horizon. Kelovin never managed to win a single duel. Their last duel left him kneeling on the floor panting. Sweat poured from his face. His arms felt like they would fall off if he tried to lift them once more.

Ryga leaned against a tree breathing normally. He looked like he had only been walking for the last couple of hours. "Prince Kelovin, it is time for you to retire. We have a long day ahead of us. I would like to leave at first light." Ryga did not wait for him to answer before leaving. Kelovin was left alone to catch his breath. Once he did, he went south past the throne once more to his sleeping area.

His bed was beneath a large tree. The grass beneath it had been manipulated to grow thick making it soft enough to count as a bed. The old tree's roots emerged from the ground on either side of the bed to create a small alcove around him where he slept. Kelovin sat against the tree. He was not ready to sleep, though it was getting late. There was still too much swimming around in his head at the moment. For a few moments, he'd had the possibility of greatness given to him, only for it to be taken away again. Perhaps Ryga had told the truth when he said he would not balk at the first sign of danger. The more he thought about it, the more his hope overcame his common sense. It told him Ryga would not truly hold him back. They would go on all the adventures he had hoped for. Their oath was simply for his protection. He let the idea swim around his mind for a while.

When he still wasn't tired, Kelovin decided he could not sit waiting for sleep to come. Kelovin rose and headed for the Great Spring. It was harder to pick his way through Bigor Forest in the black of night. His eyes only allowed him to see in the dark to a certain extent. Coming into view of the spring brought light. The moon was full tonight, reflecting its light off the still waters of the Great Spring. The area around the pond was covered in plush grass similar to his bed. Within the water, there were no fish or any other signs of living things. Being their major source of water, the Elves kept it clean by making sure nothing occupied it. On a clear, sunny day its bottom could be seen clearly, six feet down.

During the night it was impossible to see through the surface. It was like black glass stretching out before him.

"I thought you might come here as well," Pelmor said, startling him from his thoughts. Pelmor sat by the side of the spring twirling a stick around in his hand. Ever since they were little, this was where they would go to play. As they grew older, it was the spring they would sneak to at night after everyone else was asleep. Kelovin wondered how long he had been waiting there. "The spring has always been a great place to think," Pelmor said, inviting him with a hand gesture to take a seat.

"You couldn't sleep either?" Kelovin asked while he sat down next to Pelmor. He could feel the cool breeze coming off the spring's waters. His reflection stared back at him from the water's edge.

"No," Pelmor sighed. The sigh was an indication he was in the mood to have a serious conversation. They seldom had them, although Kelovin did enjoy the moments when they talked seriously. Pelmor took a deep breath, "We are about to have the craziest experience of our lives. Stuff we only ever talked about—unless you count pretending to do it as kids."

"Yeah, I know," Kelovin admitted. "Yet, perhaps not as crazy as we originally thought." Pelmor's head snapped around to look right at him. He raised an eyebrow. When he didn't say anything Kelovin explained, "Ryga made me give the blood oath to him saying I would obey his every command, never reveal my identity, and never leave his presence unless told to do so."

"Are you serious?" Pelmor said, his eyes getting wider. Pelmor's mouth opened as if he was about to say something more, but nothing came out. Kelovin nodded his head to affirm his answer. They sat silently to let it sink in. Pelmor was the first to break the silence. "Well, even so, perhaps it will still be an experience to remember even if it is not as crazy as I had been thinking."

"Which is precisely what I've been telling myself ever since Ryga made me take the oath. I want to believe we'll be out there longer than a week. I honestly don't think we will. Or we will be tourists seeing the sights, doing nothing of any importance," Kelovin said.

"Well, I wanted you to know, no matter what happens on our journey you can count on me to back you up. Ryga or no, we will become as great as Beldon. You will see," Pelmor said. There was an unspoken brotherhood between Kelovin and Pelmor. Their friendship had grown tremendously over the years. They had been through a great deal together.

"Excuse me, Pelmor. May I speak to my son for a moment, please?" a voice from directly behind them spoke.

Pelmor and Kelovin both scrambled to their feet. Pelmor made a deep bow before he said, "Whatever you wish, Queen Amylia. I was about to leave anyway."

"Thank you, Pelmor. You are a great friend to my son. I expect you will keep him safe in your travels," Kelovin's mother said.

"I'll do my best," Pelmor smiled. Pelmor turned to Kelovin. They clasped forearms with one hand and shoulders with the other hand before Pelmor turned back the way he came.

"I hope you did not plan on leaving for an indeterminate amount of time without saying goodbye," his mother said once Pelmor was gone.

"I would never. You were next on my list," Kelovin said running his hand through his hair. He found himself frowning, so he quickly replaced it with a smile. He had, indeed, forgotten to visit her. It would not do to let his mother know it.

She returned his smile. “If that’s the story you’re going with, I’ll play along,” she said.

“How did you get Father to agree to let me leave?” Kelovin asked.

“I had nothing to do with it,” she said.

“Don’t even try to pretend. I know Father would never have decided this on his own,” Kelovin said. His mother had been intervening for him with his father ever since he could remember. If it hadn’t been for her, he most likely would have been chained to a tree for the rest of his life so his father could keep an eye on him.

“I simply suggested it would do you good to learn for yourself what the outside world was like,” his mother said.

“Can’t you get him to release me from my blood oath to Ryga?” Kelovin asked.

“It was my idea to have you make an oath, even if it is the only reason your father agreed. I may want you to be able to do the things you wish, but I also want you to come back in one piece.”

“The rules I was forced to swear will not let me do what I want. It will be worse than staying here,” Kelovin said. He was careful not to let his frustration show in his voice. He would never speak to his mother in anger. He loved her too much.

“Don’t be so dramatic, Kelovin. I have spoken with Ryga. He has assured me he will show you what a real journey is like.”

Kelovin had no doubt his father had also spoken personally with Ryga. His mother’s interference was something, at least. Kelovin closed his eyes while he took a deep breath. “I’m going to miss you, Mother,” he said.

“And I shall miss you.” She paused for a moment as though she was trying to decide what to say. “Kelovin, it’s important for you to find whatever it is you’ve been searching for and return ready to be the prince your father needs you to be. Do not fail your father. Otherwise, I won't be able to ease the burden between you two anymore."

Kelovin let her words sink in for a moment before saying, "And you? Do you want me to come back ready to be a prince?"

His mother's face softened. She reached a hand out to gently stroke his cheek. "You know you're my son no matter what, but, yes, I would like you to come back ready to be a prince."

Kelovin looked to the ground, running his hand through his hair. He did not want to disappoint his mother. He looked back up at her, "Okay, Mother, as long as we actually go do something, I will obey whatever Father says when I get back."

"Kelovin, you are being sent to take care of a real problem. Your father has been talking about needing a god artifact. He is entrusting a vital mission to your hands because he believes you can do it."

Kelovin found his mouth hanging open. "This isn't you trying to make him sound better again, is it?" he asked.

"No, this is a serious matter," his mother reached out to stroke his cheek again. "Now, get some sleep. Come back safely, my darling." His mother turned away. He watched her leave before going to his tree again.

Kelovin did not find it hard to fall asleep the second time he arrived at his bed. His mother's words had calmed many of his worries. There was once more hope he would achieve the greatness he'd always dreamed of, but he certainly still had his doubts. It was only seconds before exhaustion took over.

Chapter Two

Kelovin awoke to Ryga shaking him. From the dark surrounding him, he could tell it was well before the sun would begin to rise in the sky. "Kelovin, we must leave while the city still sleeps," Ryga whispered to him. Kelovin rose groggily from the grass. A yawn escaped him as he stretched out. He could feel his muscles protest. Yesterday's training had taken its toll on him. They walked silently toward the Great Spring where they planned to meet Pelmor. He felt his heart beat faster. His arms became restless. The time had finally come for him to see the world. He was going to prove himself a great adventurer.

It occurred to him that the opposite of what he expected was possible. He might go out and find himself face-to-face with something he couldn't handle. He could end up being murdered. He found himself doubting whether this journey had been a good idea in the first place. He felt the urge to go tell his father he no longer wished to leave. The thought of continuing life under his father's eye was all it took to banish those doubts.

Pelmor waved when they came into view. He was carrying a large bag upon his back. It bulged from every side. No doubt, it was full of things for their journey. At his side was a long sword, Pelmor's weapon of preference. He wore traveling boots made of sturdy leather. At his feet was a similar bag to the one he was carrying. Kelovin assumed it must be for him. "This bag is yours, it's filled with everything we are going to need," Ryga confirmed for him, "Pick it up and let's hurry through the Sleeping Trees."

Kelovin grabbed the bag. It was heavy. He heaved it onto his shoulders despite the continued protests of his aching muscles. The edge of the Sleeping Trees was noticeably different from the rest of the forest. They became similar to the orchards the humans planted for food. They were not in the same uniform lines, yet it was easy to tell they did not grow in a natural arrangement. Walking through the Sleeping Trees without anyone there gave Kelovin an uncomfortable feeling. Knowing all of the Elves were within the trees surrounding him made it worse. He felt as though they could all emerge from the trees to attack them without warning. He knew it was ridiculous. They would never attack their own kind, especially the prince. However, knowing that did not stop his brain from imagining things.

"Have you ever been to the other side of the Sleeping Trees?" Pelmor whispered to Kelovin. Even the whisper sounded loud in the silence

"Be quiet, I don't want to wake up anyone," Kelovin hissed, bringing his finger to his lips for emphasis. Pelmor smiled, amused by the gesture.

"Do not worry. They will not hear you while they are asleep, it is not possible. Only the ones awake would be able to. No need to worry about them. They would know you're here regardless of whether or not we spoke," Pelmor told him, still smiling. He raised his voice with every word to illustrate his point.

"Then why did you whisper?" Kelovin asked, still not convinced.

"I don't know. I guess it was instinctive to whisper when it is so quiet out here," he answered, indicating their dark surroundings. Ryga held up his hand to silence both of them. The walk soon became monotonous. The Sleeping Trees expanded ahead of them, seemingly forever, with no end in sight. He had known it was a large area, he had never imagined it could stretch for so many miles. After a little over an hour of walking, he was beginning to think it would truly never end. Before bringing it up with Ryga, he noticed the forest ahead changed back to its normal way of growth. The sun was beginning to peek over the horizon when they left the Sleeping Trees. Kelovin thought it was too coincidental; Ryga must have timed their departure to it. Sunrise was typically when most Elves woke up for the day, after all.

They continued walking through the forest without speaking. He'd never realized how large their city was. He felt something didn't add up but wasn't sure what. Kelovin pondered upon it while they walked. When he felt his stomach growl in hunger, it came to him. "How do we feed all of those Elves without any kind of storage or anything?" Kelovin asked.

Ryga made a *tsk*ing noise before saying, "Kelovin you are supposed to have learned these things already. In the high branches of all the Sleeping Trees, fruit is magically grown for each Elf. As you well know, Elves do not eat meat often, only as much as is necessary. For the little we do eat, the forest itself helps keep the surroundings of our city full of things to hunt. Our relationship with the forest has grown into a significantly strong one over the years. The natural abilities of the trees combined with our magic make this place an enchanted forest. You'll never find another one like this one."

"We're taught this growing up, Kelovin," Pelmor teased. "Maybe you should have been paying more attention rather than daydreaming about heroes." Kelovin gave him a friendly shove in response.

"All right, enough," Ryga demanded. "We need to start going at a faster pace. There is an extraordinary amount of ground to cover before we reach the human city." Pelmor and Kelovin nodded their understanding. Ryga took off at a brisk jog. He kept a fast enough pace to make it necessary to concentrate on where they were going, but not fast enough for it to be hard to keep up. Kelovin wanted to talk to Pelmor. Unfortunately, he had never mastered the ability to talk and run at the same time. After hours of running, Kelovin found himself thankful for all the drills he'd done growing up. Ryga showed no indication he planned to slow down anytime soon.

When the sun had risen high above them, Ryga stopped for lunch. Kelovin immediately threw himself to the ground. He put his hand to his heart. It was trying to beat its way out of his chest. He'd been expecting a rest hours ago. Pelmor was beside him, also panting. "Why do we have to go so long without stopping?" Kelovin asked.

"This is the pace Elvin soldiers use when going on a mission. We have too much ground to cover to waste time lazing about," Ryga said.

Kelovin decided to leave the subject. Instead, he took the opportunity to look around. He'd never been this far away from Reshyr before.

Their surroundings were still the same as they had been when they'd started. Large trees rose high above them. Soft grass lay beneath them. A small stream flowed beside them toward a large river still ahead of them. Kelovin knew it was there from all the maps he would look at when he yearned for adventure. Kelovin bent down next to it to cup a few mouthfuls of water to his mouth. Pelmor must have thought it was a good idea because he got up to drink some water as well. Ryga took out three small portions of dried meat for their lunch, along with some vegetable sandwiches.

"How far do we have to travel before we pass the Elvin outposts?" Kelovin directed his question to Ryga.

Ryga did not immediately answer; instead, he finished handing out each of their rations. Once he was seated in a comfortable position he said, "The Elvin outposts stretch far across this forest. We won't be beyond them until we cross into centaur territory."

"I have never seen a centaur before," Pelmor exclaimed with excitement.

"Nor will you, if things go the way they should," Ryga said sharply. "I don't want either of you to be trying to spot any of them when we are passing through. We have an agreement with them, so they will leave us alone."

"Well, this trip isn't proving to be any fun," Pelmor sulked.

"No one ever said doing these things was fun. The grandeur of adventure is some fantasy children like to make up. This isn't like the make-believe you played as children. Now eat your lunch so we can keep moving." Ryga took a large bite of his own vegetable sandwich.

Pelmor directed his attention toward Kelovin. He spoke between mouthfuls, "Centaurs are supposed to have amazing strength, which makes it hard to fight them in single combat, especially because their hooves function as permanent weapons. You think they will come out to meet us anyway?"

"It would be pretty awesome to finally meet a centaur after having had to learn so much about them." Kelovin let his mind imagine what one would look like. He saw handsome men with more muscles than was natural. It would be awesome to see one up close. Ryga would never let them seek the centaurs out, so he would have to pin his hopes on the unlikelihood of the centaurs coming to them. He stuffed some of his sandwich into his mouth. He didn't know what was worse, the blandness of the food or how hard it was to chew. It was nothing like the fruit he was used to eating at home. Bad food wasn't a big deal. He could sacrifice a few things to be able to be away from his home.

Ryga finished his lunch with a brush of his hands. He rose from the ground to pack things away again. In a few short minutes, he was telling them to finish up so they could get moving again. Pelmor slumped against the tree he was sitting by. He groaned, "Can't we rest a bit longer?"

"Not if we want to make good time, which I do, so let's go," Ryga said. Pelmor groaned again; he got up anyway, so Kelovin did too. Once their backpacks were secured to their backs, Ryga set off at the same pace as before.

The rest of their day was as uneventful as the first part. Ryga had kept them going even a little past dark before stopping to set up camp by a small pond. He put Pelmor to the task of cooking something to eat. Kelovin was instructed to follow him a little way off from the campsite.

"Prince Kelovin, it is time we try to teach you once more to do some magic," Ryga said, staring at him as if daring him to say something about it. Kelovin sighed, already exasperated with today's lesson. They had been trying to teach him Elvin magic his whole life. He had never been able to do it once in all those years. Ryga closed his eyes a moment. He took a deep breath before saying, "Kelovin, you are an Elf, so the ability must be within you. You have to concentrate and access it. Don't give up before we begin."

"Perhaps I was a defect. Perhaps I don't even have magic. Would it be a big deal if I didn't?" Kelovin tried his normal excuses. Ryga continued to stare at him, unmoving, until defeated, Kelovin finally muttered, "Fine."

"Take a seat," Ryga commanded. As soon as Kelovin complied, Ryga continued to give him instructions, "Now, close your eyes. Let your mind reach out to those things around you."

He did as he was told. This part was easy. Ryga wanted him to find the energy sources of the plant life around him. It was the energy they drew from to do their magic. He had always been able to feel the energy but never able to tap into it.

"All right, Prince Kelovin, now I want you to emit your will to the energies around you to make this grass grow longer. Focus your mind on manipulating the energy you feel." Kelovin exerted his mind toward the life sources in vain. They would not respond to his pleadings. He kept trying until it felt like his mind would explode.

"I can't do it Ryga. They do not respond to my will. It won't ever happen."

"Yes, you can. You must. Keep trying." Kelovin sat trying for over an hour before Ryga finally relented, "We will pick this up again later. For now, we shall return to camp. It would seem our food is ready."

The air was mixed with the smells of dinner. It made his stomach growl greedily. When Pelmor saw them approaching, he said, "I decided to make some soup. It's not very full, though." He offered up a bowl of it to Kelovin. His words proved to be true. The soup held only a few bits of the same kinds of vegetables they'd eaten in their sandwich earlier in the day. What it lacked in substance, it made up for in spices. It looked like Pelmor had started dumping them in without control. Kelovin took a hesitant spoonful of it. It turned out to be one of the most delicious things he'd ever eaten.

"Thanks, Pelmor. This tastes amazing," Kelovin praised him.

"Thanks, but I'm sure it's the exhaustion talking. There wasn't much to make it with," Pelmor said as he laughed. Kelovin shrugged. His exhaustion probably did have something to do with it. He had been so hungry he probably would have thought it tasted amazing even if they were eating grass. Kelovin devoured what remained without taking time to talk any further between his mouthfuls.

"Is there more?" Kelovin asked, holding his empty bowl out toward Pelmor.

"No, I'm afraid there wasn't much to begin with, sorry," Pelmor answered, staring down at the empty pot with a frown.

"Pelmor, it is time for you to train your magic," Ryga interjected before they could begin talking about anything else.

"Okay, sounds great," Pelmor said rising from the ground as fast as he could, the lack of food already forgotten. Magic was the one thing Kelovin envied Pelmor for. Pelmor had always been one of the best of his age at magic. Kelovin was always the worst; he had never been able to do a single thing. He watched as Ryga instructed him to create a force shield. Ryga picked up a club. He struck at Pelmor repeatedly. Every time the club would stop a foot and a half away from Pelmor, almost as if it was doing it of its own accord. Yet, as the blows kept coming he could see Pelmor struggling to continue holding it up. Ryga must have noticed too because he pounded at it harder.

He was surprised when Pelmor jumped back, letting down his shield right before one of Ryga's attacks connected. Ryga's momentum carried him forward into the ground. There was a soft thud when his club slammed against it. Pelmor wasted no time. He pulled out a dagger, advancing on him. Ryga was faster. Vines shot out from the surrounding trees. They wrapped tightly around Pelmor's arms and legs. He tried to free himself. It was no use. The magical vines were too strong.

"Good work, Pelmor," Ryga told him, "Now, let's move on to the next exercise."

Their next exercise was levitating various things through a path chosen by Ryga. Once Pelmor had done it with expertise several times, Ryga moved on to manipulating the vines. Except in special circumstances, the vines were used whenever they magically manipulated a living thing inside Bigor Forest. The trees would not allow for much beyond the use of vines because they did not like to be disturbed from their rest often. Trying to force them beyond what they wanted to do would break the pact held between trees and Elves for millennia. Ryga and Pelmor did their exercises until the stars had fully emerged into the clear night.

Ryga approached Kelovin with a sad look. Kelovin could guess what he was going to ask him next. "Prince Kelovin, might you try to find rest within the trees again?" The question brought a mixture of shame and anger. The anger came from all the years he had not been able to do what Ryga was asking him to try. Every Elf in the city was able to do it, yet he could not. It was embarrassing, not to mention how it isolated him from everyone else even more. He gave a nod though he knew it was pointless to try.

"You remember how to do it, I imagine?" Ryga said it more as a question than a statement. Kelovin nodded again. He closed his eyes. He could feel the life essence of the tree next to him clearly. He tried to apply the magic he was told would allow him to communicate with its will. Nothing happened– like every other time he had tried before.

"It's no use," Kelovin admitted, letting his head slump forward.

"No matter, you will be safe enough out here. The trees will wake us if there is any harm coming this way. We must rest now. Tomorrow will be another day of long travel." Ryga walked to a tree. He disappeared as his body merged into the tree's will. That was another thing they had Beldon the Great to thank for. He had found the secret of the trees' intelligence. Once he knew it was there, he had created the pact between the trees to allow Elves to sleep within them.

Pelmor sat next to Kelovin, grinning like a hyena. “Did you see it?” Pelmor asked. The way he was fidgeting made it seem like he was going to explode with joy.

“See what?” Kelovin asked even though he had an idea of what Pelmor was talking about already.

“I almost had him!” Pelmor said. Somehow, his grin got wider.

“All I saw was you wrapped up in a bunch of vines,” Kelovin said, examining his fingernails as if he wasn’t interested in what Pelmor was saying.

“So you did see it,” Pelmor said pumping his fist in the air as if he had won something. “I don’t get how he was able to react so fast,” Pelmor said.

“I know, it was incredible,” Kelovin said, now grinning as well. “Ryga must have cast the magic the instant you jumped out of the way. He must have some crazy-good reflexes.”

“I’m going to have to move even faster next time,” Pelmor said, getting back up from the ground.

“Yeah, or be able to predict the future,” Kelovin said.

Pelmor walked to a tree; before he went in, he turned back to Kelovin. He gave him a sympathetic look. “I’m sorry you must stay out here by yourself. I’ll see you in the morning,” he whispered. Kelovin shrugged. Seconds later, Pelmor disappeared within the tree. Kelovin lay down upon the soft grass. He shifted his body until he found a comfortable spot. Sleep came easily.

They were up traveling again as the sun’s first rays peeked over the horizon. Kelovin hoped the day would bring more interesting events. He became convinced he would be sorely disappointed again with every hour passing. The day dragged on exactly as the first one had. Ryga kept their pace at a jog most of the day. Kelovin decided he no longer cared if they kept up such a rigorous pace because it meant they would arrive at their destination faster, or perhaps, to some point of their journey more exciting than what they were doing now.

When there wasn't much time left before the sun would disappear again, they found a small clearing to make the day's camp. Pelmor whispered to him as they stopped, "I don't know why, but it looks like he isn't making us go as long today."

"It probably means he wants to practice harder," Kelovin whispered back. It would be like Ryga to find ways to work them harder. The clearing was an area where a few trees had died long ago. Something must have prevented new ones from growing in their place. Dead branches were littered everywhere, making it easy to gather wood for the fire. He and Pelmor were assigned to building the fire.

Kelovin and Pelmor found the task to be harder than they imagined. Pelmor was muttering to himself as he tried getting a spark to catch fire. A moment later, Pelmor stood up and cursed loudly as he threw the stick as far away as he could. When he noticed Kelovin staring at him, he muttered, "Stupid stick didn't want to light." Pelmor picked up a new stick and went back to work.

"So, does this great adventure of yours sound as awesome now?" Pelmor said in his playful tone as their efforts to start the fire continued in vain. Kelovin knew his remark could only mean Pelmor was regretting having been dragged into this journey.

"It has only been two days. There is still plenty of time for us to do great things as we planned. We have to be more patient than we anticipated," Kelovin answered calmly.

"Are you going to be saying the same thing after three months have passed and we still haven't done anything worth mentioning?" Pelmor asked in a way that he could argue was only a thought, nothing more. Kelovin knew better. What he was really saying was, *I can't believe you dragged me on this stupid quest of yours. I'm going to suffer for a long time until you realize there is nothing fun about this.* Kelovin became slightly annoyed.

"Why can't you use your stupid magic to light the fire," he said a little more harshly than he intended.

"Whoa, no need to get so angry. I was only discussing what might happen," Pelmor said, playing it off as though he never had a problem with anything.

"Sorry, it's because I hate how long it takes to start a fire," Kelovin grimaced. He hated apologizing even more when he knew Pelmor had not only been "discussing things." He valued his friendship with Pelmor far more than being right in some argument, so he did not pursue the matter.

"Fire is kind of a tricky thing with our magic. It takes too much energy to create it, so not many can." Kelovin nodded as though he had not already known the fact. They worked on in silence trying various methods to make it light, but the rotting wood did not want to burn. It was dark by the time they had the fire going well enough to cook some food. Dinner was to be the same stew as yesterday.

"Something is wrong," Ryga said as they prepared the food. He rose from the ground reaching for his sword; it was already too late.

"You're surrounded by archers, if you try to do anything at all you will be shot down," a voice called out from the edge of the trees.

"Show yourself," Ryga commanded. He did not seem to be worried at all. A large centaur walked into the clearing. The centaur stood at nearly eight-feet-tall on all fours. His horse half was armored with a bright steel plate, except where it would prohibit mobility. Those bare spots revealed dark black hair. From his torso up, he wore no armor. His body rippled with muscles. His hair was the same dark black color. It fell most of the way down his back. In his hand, he held a bastard sword worn from constant usage.

Anger far greater than Kelovin had ever remembered seeing in Ryga became evident in the sudden change in his posture. His hands clenched around the hilt of his sword, his body leaned forward ready to spring, his eyes narrowed. Through clenched teeth he spoke, "What do you think you're doing? Have you forgotten the centuries of peace we have shared with each other?"

"Peace was broken the second your lot began poisoning our water supply," The centaur roared flaring his nostrils.

The tension in Ryga's body left. His eyebrows furled together, "Poisoned your water supply? What do you mean?"

"Do not play innocent with me, Elf. Your part of the river is upstream from us. We have not heard of any of you dying from poisoned water, so you have to be the ones ruining the water supply," he accused them. He apparently did not know they got all of their water from the natural spring within their city. Only Elves were allowed to enter the city; outsiders were strictly forbidden. So, Kelovin did not blame him for not knowing. The centaur continued his accusations, "We have been suffering immensely. We were on our way to confront your king on the matter. I have a better idea now. It seems to me, if we take his son captive it will be a much greater bargaining chip."

"I think you are mistaken on more than one thing, Centaur," Ryga had recovered his composure completely. "We do not go to the river for a water supply, so our lack of suffering does not automatically implicate fault. You are also mistaken about our identities. We are scouts doing our rounds. However, we would be happy to let you be on your way to speak with the king in a peaceful manner if you have any inclination to keep the peace we have shared for so long."

"Make no mistake, Elf, I am no fool. I know who you are. You are no scout. This lad looks to be old enough to be the king's son. There is no other reason you would be this far from the king since you are his right-hand servant. Surrender now, and no one will get hurt," the centaur said. While he spoke, Kelovin searched the night sky as he remembered some of his lessons about the centaur culture. He needed to find a specific grouping of stars.

"Are you willing to initiate a war over something we did not even do?" Ryga asked, perplexed at the centaur's determination to blame them.

"No, we are not. We are willing to go to war against you for the crimes we are certain you have committed," he replied.

"May I ask your name?" Kelovin spoke up without warning.

The centaur regarded him as one would a small child trying to talk about adult things. "So, the young thing speaks as well. It was rude of me not to introduce myself. My name is Jorga, son of Torg, Chief of the Stargazers. Now stay out of a conversation best left to the big boys." Kelovin thought the centaur looked no older than he was. Centaurs did not live as long as Elves, yet he did not imagine it meant they matured faster.

He decided to ignore the insult. "Jorga, look to the sky. The warrior is bright today. I would challenge you to a battle of truth to settle this. The battle shall prove our innocence of these crimes you speak of." Centaurs believed whenever the warrior was in the sky a battle between two warriors seeking for truth would leave only the one speaking the truth left standing.

Jorga threw his head back with deep laughter, "I commend you on your knowledge of our customs and your bravery. I promise you it will be the last act of bravery you'll ever make. I will accept your challenge." Ryga made no move to interfere. Kelovin drew his sword confidently. Jorga rushed him at a gallop, leaving Kelovin with no other choice except to dive out of his way. The centaur stopped his gallop to turn on him. Kelovin was not prepared for how easily Jorga managed it. Kelovin scrambled to his feet in time to parry a vicious overhead swing. The force caused his knees to quiver. Fear swept over him. Perhaps his quick decision had gotten him into more than he could handle this time. He did not remember a time when he had been truly fearful for his life. He'd always been well-protected within the city. Now, fear gripped him tight. Only the constant lessons from Ryga allowed him to not let it take away from his fighting. He danced to the side, away from Jorga, to buy himself a couple of precious seconds to regroup. Jorga proved not to be easily evaded, turning to face him as if he had two legs rather than four.

Kelovin knew he couldn't let the fight last for long. He could not match the strength of a centaur. He went in swinging two quick slashes high, then spun into a slash toward his lower gut. Jorga was not quick enough to parry the third, so instead, he swung his rear around into it. Kelovin's attack glanced off the steel plate he wore. Jorga went back on the offensive, but he did not have the time to make his attack as strong as the first one.

Sweat poured down his face as he tried to find an opening in the centaur's defense. Every time Kelovin took advantage of an opening in Jorga's attacks, Jorga would turn his steel plate into it, glancing his blows away easily. He jumped back from the fight once more, this time Jorga did not pursue right away. Kelovin knew what he must do to win the fight. He had to surprise the centaur, throwing him off his balance. With Jorga's speed and strength, it did not look to be a likely possibility.

Kelovin focused on summoning as much strength as he could to his arms, willing it to be more than he was capable of. He charged Jorga, going into a sideways swing like what would be seen from someone wielding a club. Though Jorga had not been expecting such a wild attack, he was able to move to parry in time. When their swords connected, Kelovin's attack hit with such force it shattered Jorga's blade, causing him to fall on his hindquarters. The shock of what he did might have stopped him had he been sparring with Ryga. The adrenaline pumping through him helped him continue fighting. He drew his arms overhead to thrust one final blow into Jorga's chest.

"Kelovin, stop," Ryga commanded sternly. Kelovin's arms were already moving through the attack. It was too late to obey. A sudden invisible force met his thrust shoving it sideways into the centaur's arm. Jorga cried out in pain. Around them, shouts of confusion echoed as vines took hold of the centaurs, circling them. Kelovin barely heard any of it. He was shouting in agony upon the ground. His whole body felt as though it was being stabbed simultaneously by thousands of long knives. Thoughts of battle left his mind completely. The pain was unbearable. Then it was gone as suddenly as it had come.

Ryga was standing over him. Kelovin looked up at him searching for an answer through the lingering pain. Ryga supplied him with an explanation, "The pain is what happens when you break an oath, Kelovin. Your body is seized with pain until you no longer intend to disobey. I stopped you because it would do us no good to kill the chief's son. It would only further cause this war we do not wish to start." Ryga turned his attention to Jorga who had pulled the sword from his shoulder. He tossed it aside as if it were a toy. "Jorga, you have your battle of truth. You were the loser which indicates we are telling the truth. Now, take your centaurs and leave."

It was only after Jorga gave his slight nod of confirmation that Ryga released the other centaurs from his spell. They all quietly left, heading back toward their own territory. It would have been a grave insult to their gods had they continued to oppose them after a battle of truth. Kelovin still lay upon the ground, the memory of such agonizing pain in his mind. “Sleep. It will make you feel better,” Ryga told him. He did not have to be told twice. His body welcomed the sleep; he needed it to recover from the blood oath’s punishment.

The next morning, he awoke to Pelmor nudging him awake. “Ryga says it’s time for us to get moving.” Kelovin rubbed the sleep from his eyes. He sat up to take a look around. Sitting up made his entire body groan. Everything was packed away already. Ryga was nowhere to be seen. Pelmor handed him some fruit, which made Kelovin realize he was starving. Pelmor waited a moment while Kelovin devoured the fruit before asking, “Are you okay? Yesterday was pretty insane—the fight with the centaur and all.”

Memories of what happened the night before came flooding back into his mind. He had no idea how he had done those things. “I think I’m okay now,” Kelovin said. He did not feel any real pain, yet, somehow, the memory of it still made his body ache.

“How’d you do it last night?” Pelmor asked with awe. “I mean, shatter the centaur’s blade.”

“I don’t know. I guess I’m stronger than I thought,” Kelovin grinned, unsure himself where the strength had come from.

“Shattering his blade wasn’t the only crazy thing happening yesterday, either. While you fought with Jorga, your hair became a darker gold than normal. I know it sounds insane. It was clearly noticeable, my friend.” Kelovin couldn’t detect any hint of sarcasm in his voice nor in his face. He shrugged, not knowing what happened either. Then he remembered he’d missed his mark with his thrust.

"What happened, why did my thrust falter?" Kelovin asked.

"Ryga created a force shield to protect Jorga," Pelmor answered.

"Then why didn't he create one to stop the attack completely? Why still let it pierce his shoulder?" Kelovin asked.

"Because your attack had far greater force behind it than I anticipated, so what I created wasn't enough to stop it," Ryga explained emerging from the trees. "You would have launched a war between two races who have shared peace for over a millennium by killing Jorga. Where was your brain last night, Kelovin?" Ryga did not show anger, only irritation. It told Kelovin Ryga had been completely in control of the situation. There had been no way he was going to actually kill Jorga.

"I'm sorry Ryga. Does this mean we are heading back to the city?"

"No, it has only been two sunrises since we left. It would not look good to return so soon. It does mean we will be changing our course. We will head south in order to go around the centaur territory." Ryga handed him his sword. There was a small chip in the sword where he had hit Jorga's blade.

"I must admit, I was surprised you let me fight him," Kelovin said.

"It was a good idea to declare a battle of truth. It left them no room to argue when you emerged the victor. Besides, Jorga knew you were worth more to him alive than dead, so he would not have killed you. Even if he had tried, I was prepared to stop him. I must send word of all of this back to the king." They were able to send messages to anywhere within the forest by using the trees. Their wills were all connected in a way that let them share information instantaneously. Thinking about it made him certain it would be unwise for the centaurs to fight the Elves within Bigor

Forest. Ryga turned toward the trees once more to send his message.

Pelmor resumed talking to him once Ryga was busy, "Whatever it was you did, it was awesome. Jorga was huge, much stronger than I'd imagined. Yet, you still laid him on his hindquarters."

"I couldn't believe it myself. I had so much adrenaline pumping through me, I was about to explode." This was the kind of thing Kelovin had been waiting for. His confidence in their adventure was renewed. If this was what happened with the centaurs, he couldn't wait for what lay ahead. Kelovin looked at Pelmor with a smile, "I bet you're glad we came out now, after all."

"Yeah, I must admit it was more excitement than I ever expected to get into. Best of all, Ryga said we aren't turning back. Maybe we were wrong about him. Maybe he actually does want to you to experience great things."

Ryga returned with his bag on his shoulders. "It's time to go." Kelovin and Pelmor looked happily at each other, sharing each other's excitement.

They traveled four days before reaching Bigor's edge. Before them lay a field of grass that came up to their thighs. Kelovin had never seen anything like it.

"You can see forever," Pelmor gasped. There were barely any trees to block their vision, letting them see for nearly a mile. Kelovin swept his gaze across the field, taking it all in. Then he spotted a village. He had never seen so many buildings in one spot. Many of them were made out of wood. It was a strange sight. He wanted to go explore it all.

"Ryga, let's go to the village," he said.

"No, you two will stay here. I am going to go to the village to purchase some horses. Stay hidden. I don't want anyone to see you while I'm gone."

"All right," Kelovin agreed, though he did not want to. He was not about to experience the pain of disobeying Ryga's orders again. Once was enough to learn his lesson. Ryga left them on the forest's edge.

"Horses will be able to go far faster on a field like this," Pelmor observed. Kelovin had no arguments with his logic. It was good they had come upon a village; they would be able to make it to the human city far faster. Then, Ryga would not be able to make him stay out. He would have to go in. Then he would be able to see what it was like. He told himself he needed to remember to thank his father whenever it was they returned. This journey was already turning out to be great.

Chapter Three

Ryga led them as he usually did, keeping his horse several paces ahead of them. Kelovin and Pelmor rode side by side. They did not mind Ryga riding in front. It left the two of them to talk freely together. Their day had barely started and Kelovin was already becoming restless from the day's journey. He wanted to stop to rest a while. He had to dig deep to find the energy to make himself keep moving. There was no telling when Ryga would decide to take a break. It was impossible to see a pattern in the Elf's decisions. Their surroundings didn't make for a great resting place anyway. The grass was tall in this part of the land, nearly coming up to the necks of their horses. Kelovin wondered if there were any bones of small children who'd been lost in the endless stuff. Worst of all, there weren't any trees to shade them.

"I had no idea great adventures took so much traveling. We haven't even started the searching part yet," Pelmor was saying, "I wish we would get there so we can get this mission underway." It was at the human city they planned to find information on possible locations for one of the god artifacts. It was rumored each of the four gods had their own special artifact they bestowed on those they deemed worthy of the honor.

"Why do all of the races have the same four gods?" Kelovin asked, changing the subject. It was strange for so many races to worship the same people when each race was so different from one another. If the Gods were truly all the same, then Kelovin did not understand how the Gods could love the Elves the same as the humans. It just did not make any sense.

"They're not all exactly the same," Pelmor began to answer. Pelmor had been showing an intelligent side of himself that Kelovin had never seen while growing up. It was hard to believe because he knew how little attention Pelmor and he had given to their lessons, at least while he was around. "Each race has changed the gods to their own imaginations, eventually giving them their own names. It is said, once long ago, we all lived together in harmony with the same four gods until war broke out, causing the Great Divide. From then, it was only a matter of time before they changed what the gods were to each race. Humans never remember their past for long. They do not even recall we once lived together."

None of the races Kelovin knew of had love for the humans. They were a greedy people who enjoyed war too much. Many races could not avoid having to deal with them, however, because they were skilled at having what everyone else needed. For them it was information. For others, it was essential supplies to live. Since the Great Divide, there was only one group who'd never dealt with humans again. The Dwarves of the Binal Mountains. Kelovin had never met them before, but he'd heard they were a thriving civilization with countless treasures beyond compare.

"Look," Pelmor whispered, pulling Kelovin from his thoughts. He was pointing ahead of them toward the horizon. Kelovin strained his eyes to make out what was ahead.

"A village," Kelovin said a little louder than he had intended to. Pelmor frantically waved one arm at him while making quieting motions with his finger and lips. Luckily, Ryga made no indication he had heard. They were planning on confronting Ryga about letting them go into the village before he commanded them to stay. It was the only way Kelovin would be able to avoid the pain of defying the oath he had made to Ryga. They had seen a handful of villages from afar on their journey thus far. They were never allowed to see one up close. They were always left to hide while Ryga went into the village to get supplies. Then they would go far around the village before continuing.

"Come on, let's go talk to him," Kelovin whispered, spurring his horse a little faster. Before they got there, Pelmor clutched at his side, feigning pains the best he could. Their plan was to claim he needed to see a medical man because they did not know what was wrong. They thought Ryga would be forced to let them go to the village. "Ryga, Pelmor is hurt," Kelovin called out, trying to sound as urgent as he could. Ryga turned his horse around. He rode back to meet them. The whole time Pelmor was moaning about the pain he did not have.

"What's the problem?" Ryga asked sharply.

"My stomach," Pelmor groaned.

"He has been having problems for a couple of days now. It's never been this bad. We don't know what causes it. We must see a medical man as quickly as possible," Kelovin supplied as further explanation.

Ryga stared at Pelmor for a long time, "I don't know...there is a village up ahead. Perhaps I can go explain to them what is wrong and bring back medicine for him."

"No," Kelovin said a little too quickly. "I mean, uh, I think it would be best if they saw him so they can know exactly what's wrong." Pelmor let out a moan far louder than any he had done so far. He slumped forward and fell from his horse, landing squarely on his shoulder. It was all Kelovin could do not to laugh at the dramatic flair Pelmor used while falling from his horse.

Kelovin indicated Pelmor with his hand saying, "Look at him, we have to go now."

Ryga laughed. Kelovin looked at him strangely, confused by his reaction. "Is laughing all you can do? Pelmor is in serious pain here."

"If you two want to see a village bad enough you're willing to injure yourselves, you can come. Tell Pelmor to stop pretending he's hurt—there is no need for it. If you are coming, you will do as you're told. You will talk to none of the villagers. You will do nothing unless I tell you to do so, understand?" Ryga commanded.

"Yes," they both said immediately. Pelmor rose from the ground, forgetting the terrible agony he'd pretended to have seconds before. Ryga turned his horse back around without saying anything else. Kelovin and Pelmor exchanged a look but followed happily.

"How do you think he knew?" Pelmor asked once Ryga had gained a comfortable lead in front of them.

"Most likely, because we are not half as clever as we think we are. It was a nice touch falling from your horse," Kelovin said. Seeing in his head the image of Pelmor falling to the ground made him smile.

"You think so? I was in the moment. I thought it would make things more convincing. What do you think the village will be like?" Pelmor loved to imagine things, sometimes more than he enjoyed actually doing them. They had conjured up many crazy fantasies about the villages they'd seen before. The one they liked best was that the villages were full of cannibalistic humans who would eat them alive if they were caught in their domain. It would explain why Ryga worked so hard on keeping them out.

"Probably as normal as all the other villages we passed appeared to be when we watched them from afar." In normal circumstances, Kelovin would have started making things up about the village before they got there. He didn't this time because he was afraid if he let himself get too excited about it, the disappointment would be too much for him. He had a hunch the experience was going to be as boring as every other part of their journey thus far. He could not figure out why Ryga would let them go so easily if it wasn't boring.

"Oh, don't ruin the experience before you have it," Pelmor said as if reading his thoughts. "It will be fun. At the very least, we will be able to see a human for the first time." Kelovin was discovering there was much in the world they had never seen before.

He chose not to reply to his friend's assurances; instead, he let their conversation fall to silence. The distance between them and Ryga disappeared gradually the closer they approached the village. Kelovin could not tell if it was because they rode their horses faster in excitement or if Ryga slowed his horse to keep a closer watch on the two of them. Perhaps it was both.

The houses became much larger than they looked from afar. All of them were made out of wood, which made him shudder. The logs had all been cut neatly before being stacked on each other with a mud-like substance caked in between them to hold them together. "They must have cut dozens of trees to make this many houses," he heard Pelmor whisper. The village was not large in comparison to Reshyr. Despite its small size, it still hosted more buildings than his entire city. It almost made him sick.

The sound of voices carried out across the field. He could see children outside playing. They did not look much different from the Elvin kind, perhaps, not as slender or as quick. Their ears were rounded instead of pointed as well. It did not feel like some great thing to see a human as Pelmor had thought it would be. The village was a different story. He kept looking around at it in amazement. It was strange to walk amid so many buildings made of dead trees. It made him ask himself what the city would be like if this was only a village.

The ringing of a hammer beating against metal pulled his attention elsewhere. He could hear it coming from the other side of the village.

"Ryga, I can hear a smith at work. I should go get myself a new sword here," Kelovin whispered, unsure if he should speak normally or not. One night during their travels, his sword had completely broken during practice. It had been a sad moment. He'd been fond of the weapon, mostly because Corrae had given it to him.

"Yes, we will head there shortly," Ryga assured him. Kelovin noticed the villagers had begun to stare at them passing by. It made him feel uncomfortable, sensing the villagers' eyes following their every move. He was no stranger to being stared at, as a prince. This time it felt different. He was one of the most important people in his city. When he was in Reshyr it felt as though he was loved. Here the stares felt cold, as though the three of them were there to murder everyone. He thought about what it might be like if they were humans walking within the trees of Reshyr. They probably would have been killed already. No outsiders were permitted within their city. He thanked the gods this village did not seem to hold the same feelings, even if it might seem close to it.

Ryga made his way to a farmer selling his wares on the main road of the village. The farmer was eyeing the bulging pouch at Ryga's side. His hands moved back and forth in spasms from packing things away to unpacking them again a second later. During the whole process, his eyes never moved.

"I need some food for our travels," Ryga announced. When the farmer made no move to reply he continued, pointing as he spoke, "I want a bag of potatoes and we will need at least a pound of apples and some of the dried beef as well." The things he had chosen were common among most lands.

"It will be a silver coin if you want it," the farmer grunted without looking at them.

"You're asking for more than twice what it's worth," Ryga said.

"Prices are higher for Elvin kind due to the risk of doing business with them." The farmer folded his arms across his chest. Kelovin wished he could have hit the man then. He would have as well had it not been for Ryga's commands before they entered the city. Ryga was unaffected by the man's belligerence.

"I will give you half a silver coin for it." Ryga's face remained emotionless as he spoke. It was still far more than what the food was worth. The man's face scrunched up. Kelovin assumed he must have been weighing out his options. Finally, the farmer resigned to sell his food for half a silver coin. Ryga rifled through his pouch of money and handed the man his coin. Ryga hauled the food a short distance away from the farmer before they split all of it between their backpacks.

Once Kelovin finished adjusting his own backpack, he addressed Ryga, "Why did you let him swindle us. He knew he was overcharging. He said so himself. I would have forced him to sell at the regular price."

"If I had forced him, there would have been a riot within the village. It is no secret the humans do not like us. Might I also point out the feeling is mutual, at least for most Elves, Prince Kelovin. We must tread carefully, otherwise, we will find ourselves in more trouble than we can handle. There is little trust to be found between the races, even in the human cities where there are multiple races living together," Ryga said.

"You speak as though you've seen human cities before," Kelovin said. He had not known of any Elves going out of the forest at all.

"I have a few times. You are still young, there is much you haven't seen or heard," Ryga said. Kelovin wasn't sure if he had meant it to sound as condescending as it did.

"Do other Elves live outside of Reyshyr?" Kelovin asked.

"Some do."

"I thought the king's oath made it so no one could leave the forest." Kelovin remembered the pain of breaking a blood oath with a shudder. He did not imagine anyone wanting to feel the pain of disobeying for their entire lives. Nor did he think someone could survive it past a day.

"No, Kelovin. There are three main things the king's oath does. It prevents any kind of rebellion from happening, it prevents people from disobeying his commands when he gives them a special way, and it prevents Elves from building another Elvin city to rival Reshyr. Elves in small groups living in various parts of the world pose no threat to the king. Another city, however, may eventually have its dangers." It was all supposed to be for the protection of Reshyr, but no one had dared attack their city for over a thousand years, which meant no one in Reshyr had ever experienced war. It made Kelovin wonder how well they would handle someone launching a full-scale invasion against them.

Kelovin was about to ask more when Ryga held up his hand. While talking, they had made their way over to the smith's building. It had no walls like the one in his city. It was twice as large with a great big forge within.

The smith was a burly man with the belly of a drunkard. His arms and hands were marked with numerous scars. Kelovin wondered if they were from being a smithy or from combat. The man looked up at them when they entered. He grunted and turned back to his work.

"I will give you a gold coin for a good sword for my friend here." Ryga's offer got the smith's attention faster than anything else could have.

"What kind of sword are you looking for?" the smith asked Ryga, putting down his work.

"A long sword would be our first choice," Ryga told him.

"I don't have any of them. I don't usually make swords. Not much demand for them around here. The closest I got is a bastard sword. It's a good blade. It will serve its purpose." The smith went to a rack, pulling off a sword hidden among farm tools. He handed it hilt-first to Kelovin. Kelovin took it carefully. He gave it a couple of practice swings. It was not as well done as the one Corrae had made, but it would work for now. Kelovin gave a nod.

"Very well, then, here is your gold coin. Thank you for your service," Ryga handed the man his pay. The smith grunted again and turned back to his work, pretending they had stopped existing.

"Try not to break this one as fast as the last one. If you're not careful, you could spend all our money on replacing your swords," Pelmor said, laughing.

"At least I put mine to good use," Kelovin shot back.

"What, are you saying I don't?"

"I haven't seen you do anything with one yet."

"Yeah, well, it's because I haven't had the opportunity," Pelmor stammered. Kelovin wasn't listening anymore. He was distracted by shouting coming from a long wooden building they were passing by. There was a sign hanging from above the door naming the place The Drunken Boar. He did not know what could possibly convince a man it was a good name for a store. A man walking through the door gave him a glimpse inside.

He saw many tables occupied by people with drinks in their hands. A young woman was walking around carrying other drinks to more people within the place. The shouting was coming from a table where three men sat looking to be particularly drunk. He'd only ever been taught about alcohol before. He'd never been able to see its effects, it was not allowed within the city of Reshyr.

"I would like to go into this place," Kelovin announced as the door closed. A glance toward Pelmor told him he was thinking the same thing.

"No. Taverns are not a good place to be." Ryga denied them once more. Kelovin was not surprised. It was the most common occurrence in their trek so far. They rode onward to their next destination within the village. He could smell the stables before he could see them. He couldn't help wondering why the people of the village would allow such awful-smelling things to reside within the village itself. If there had been any use for horses within Reshyr, they certainly wouldn't have been kept in a smelly, confined area and definitely not within the living area, either. He was discovering there were many differences between the human way of living and the Elvin way of living.

The building holding the horses was not large. It could not have held more than six horses at a time. When they approached, there was a boy tending to the horses. "We must speak to the stable master," Ryga stated. He waited a moment until he saw the boy was going to ignore him, much like the rest of the village. He pulled from his belt a copper coin, holding it out where the boy could easily see it. It caught the boy's attention. When he made a grab for it, Ryga pulled it back. "The stable master," Ryga repeated. The boy ran off to a nearby house. He disappeared inside, making sure to close the door behind him. When he reappeared, there was a man with black hair following behind him. Up close, he could see the man was small and scrawny with a scar across his forehead. It looked almost like the shape of a hoof.

The man looked up at them. They were obviously the last visitors he'd expected to see. He growled, "You did not tell me they were Elvin folk." Ryga ignored the obvious insult and tossed a copper coin to the boy. The boy bolted as soon as he had it in his hands.

"Good day to you, sir. We are in need of exchanging our horses for fresh ones."

"I'll trade them for three gold coins and not a coin less." The stable master held out his hand as though what he'd said was normal. Kelovin glared at him with clenched fists. If there wasn't an oath holding him back, he didn't know what he might have done. After glancing at Kelovin, the man added, "Four, because of the way your boy is staring at me. I don't like it."

"I will give you one gold coin. Our horses are healthy and young, and it is still high enough a price you will not be mocked for dealing with Elves," Ryga said.

"It still doesn't make up for this one's stares. He looks as if he would like to kill me. Not showing good manners to the man helping him out now, is he?" The man gave Kelovin a wink. It almost made Kelovin risk the pain that tearing off the man's head would cause.

"You must pardon him, he woke up angry this morning. He looks so at everyone he sees, including us." Ryga still tossed him an extra silver coin on top of the gold one they were giving for the horses.

"Very well." They were led to the stables where the man picked the three worst horses out of the six he had. Even the three worst were in better shape than theirs. Their horses all clearly needed to rest and recover from their travels.

They put the village behind them once the trade was complete. Kelovin rode with his eyes staring holes into the ground. He could not decide whether he had enjoyed the experience or not. It was great to see so many new things. On the flip side, he had never been so disrespected in his whole life.

"Your attitude cost even more coin than the high prices we normally would have had to spend," Ryga scolded him. "You must learn to swallow your pride out here. If you want to receive the help we seek, you must be willing to not act as a prince would."

"Well, I am a prince," Kelovin said, as though Ryga needed reminding of it.

"You'll die as one, too, if you don't watch how you interact with others," Ryga said. He turned his horse around and pulled it to a stop to look at Kelovin. There was a cold fire blazing in his eyes.

"I do not fear any of these people. I have far more skill than any of them have," Kelovin said. He raised his head high. He was not going to be shamed into apologizing for the rudeness of others.

"That will not always be the case, I'm afraid. There will be those you face who are stronger than you. Your pride will not serve you well then." It was annoying to hear Ryga tell him not to act like a prince after so many years of telling him to do the opposite. There was nothing he could do to win an argument against Ryga. Ryga was still in the position to send them home if Kelovin did not behave as Ryga wanted, so he nodded as to indicate he understood. Ryga must have been satisfied enough with his answer because he turned his horse back around.

There were still a few hours of daylight they could use before needing to set up camp, so they kicked their horses into a trot across the unbroken fields of grass.

They hadn't ridden for long before Kelovin got the feeling something was wrong. The wind around them had been blowing harder ever since they left the village. There was something strange about it. Kelovin could not put his finger on it. Ryga must have felt it too because he pulled his horse to a stop, motioning for them to stop as well.

"What's wrong?" Pelmor asked nervously.

"I don't know yet, there is a large presence of magic coming this way. Stay still." Ryga emitted a wave of magic, enveloping Kelovin and Pelmor. Kelovin could feel its powerful presence. Ryga talked urgently, his voice soft, "Evil is in the wind. You will stay completely still. I have laid protective spells over you. They will not permit me to hear anything you say and will hide you from whatever is coming. Kelovin, you must obey me. Do not interfere, no matter what happens. If I do not make it, you must return to Reshyr. Pelmor, you must protect Prince Kelovin with your life."

"What's wrong? What's going on?" Kelovin screamed at him. It was no use, Ryga could not hear him. Ryga had already turned his horse forward again. "Pelmor, can you tell what's happening?" Kelovin looked to his friend. One look at his face told him that even if Pelmor did know, Kelovin was not going to get an answer from him. Pelmor's face was transfixed with a look that was frightened and blank at the same time. Kelovin was frightened himself. It didn't make sense. What could possibly have caused Ryga to react so drastically? Unfortunately, he did not have to wait long to find out.

Ryga had only gone a small distance when a line of flame burst into life in front of him. His horse reared high, throwing an unsuspecting Ryga to the ground. The blue flame moved unnaturally. It burned a circle, encompassing them all without spreading through the rest of the grass.

The horse Ryga had been riding raced to escape before the fire closed in the opposite direction. Kelovin watched helplessly as it passed him and Pelmor, still mounted on their horses. It was clear Ryga's horse was oblivious to their presence. Kelovin silently willed the horse to go faster. In the end, the horse's race for freedom was too slow. The circle completed itself barely in time to trap it.

The animal tried desperately to stop itself, skidding to a halt inches away from the fire. The relief was only momentary. The blue fire leaped out, hungrily engulfing the horse in its flame. Kelovin marveled at the monstrous power this magic contained. His fears for Ryga became more substantial. He turned his attention back to where Ryga now stood waiting in the middle of the flaming circle.

Kelovin watched in disbelief as a man carried by a small cyclone of wind came straight through the flames into the circle. His hair was short with spikes. It was colored a tie-dye of dark crimson and the kind of yellow that came from sunset. His eyes blazed with a dark shade of the same fierce colors. There was a pause between the two as they stared each other down, both sizing the other one up. Tension built up in Kelovin's muscles while he waited for something to happen.

Ryga made the first move. A wave of grass came to life, twisting around the man to devour him. Kelovin hoped the match might be a short one, but then the grass burst into flames. From it the man emerged, laughing as though the attack had been child's play. Ryga had taught Kelovin it was not easy to set magical growth on fire during one of their many lessons about magic. Whoever this man was, he wielded great power.

A gust of wind drove into Ryga's chest, knocking him to the ground. The man spoke. His voice sounded menacing, with a low ominous sound to it, "It is rude to start the fight without introducing yourself to the Elf who is going kill you." The Elf's grin spread wider. Kelovin gasped. He could not believe an Elf was attacking Ryga. As far as he knew, there weren't any accounts of Elves randomly attacking one other. A closer look revealed his body to be Elvin-shaped. The Elf continued in his cold voice, "Allow me to introduce myself first. I'm called Visrim."

"Why would an Elf want to harm us?" Kelovin exclaimed in dismay. Pelmor still was not reacting to anything, however, so his words fell on deaf ears.

"Your powers are strange. I've never felt this kind of magic before. Where did you come from?" Ryga questioned him.

Visrim threw his head back and laughed at the question, "You've forgotten us already. Your kings, the ones you give your life for, have been hiding things from you, Elf. I do not have the time to explain a history to you. Now, if you will, your name, Elf."

"What is your purpose in attacking me?" Ryga asked.

"Why would I need a purpose? I'm killing you because I can. Now, for the last time your name."

"What has made you this way?" Ryga continued to question him.

"If you will not tell me your name, I will have to kill you without it." A cyclone of flames burst from Visrim's hands straight at Ryga. He protected himself with a force shield, letting the cyclone burst upon it before letting go of the shield. The ground shook slightly as Ryga levitated a host of small rocks hidden beneath the ground into the air. The rocks went flying at Visrim with enough speed to kill. Visrim countered with a strong wind causing the rocks to scatter around him.

Ryga leaped nimbly to the side, dodging the stream of blue flames Visrim sent following his gust of wind. "Let's have a little fun, shall we?" Visrim called. A sword made of pure flames grew from his hands. Ryga drew his own blade from its sheath. Visrim rushed in with a flurry of attacks. Ryga dodged them all, but Kelovin could see from Ryga's posture he was on edge. Fear was never an emotion Kelovin thought he would see in Ryga. It was clear he was not confident in his ability to win the fight.

Ryga kept dodging around the attacks until a clear opening was made. He swung at the opening, and his sword slowed in mid-swing until it stopped. It was as though Visrim had created a force shield, but it was wrong. Kelovin knew force shields did not slow attacks to a stop. They acted as a real shield would, so it couldn't have actually been a force shield.

Whatever it was, it left Ryga wide open for the flaming sword to come down on his arm. It did not cut through his arm, but the damage was done all the same. The skin around where it hit turned to charcoal. Ryga screamed as his nerves were fried. His sword fell to the ground. His arm was now useless.

Visrim continued to slash at him, but his attacks were stopped by a large force shield. Ryga took the time he created to put distance between himself and Visrim. There was anguish in Ryga's eyes. He was already wearing down, and it didn't look like Visrim had even broken a sweat.

Drops of rain started to fall from the sky. Kelovin looked up in surprise. There had not been a cloud in sight, yet now there, above them, was a massive black cloud. On the battlefield, Visrim was stalking Ryga wherever he fled.

Kelovin realized Ryga was trying to distract him from the fact he was levitating rocks behind Visrim to prepare a surprise attack. Visrim was oblivious to the rocks hurtling at his back. Ryga had finally overcome Visrim's ferocious attacks. Kelovin's heart caught in his throat when the rocks dissolved to dust, blowing around Visrim harmlessly. Visrim stopped his attacks momentarily. "How clever of you, Elf. If it weren't for my friend, you probably would have killed me. Not many can even say they've come close. You should be proud of yourself."

Kelovin searched the field for another person. He could not see any signs of someone else. A scream of pain brought his attention back to Ryga. Raindrops were turning into icicles as they fell. One had plunged straight into Ryga's shoulder. Soon, most of the raindrops were changing to ice. Fortunately, Ryga had already thrown up a shield to cover himself.

"You cannot hold it forever, Elf," Visirim taunted. He walked purposefully toward Ryga with death in his eyes. He struck at the shield with his flaming sword in long, deliberate strokes. Kelovin could see his teacher's strength failing him.

Desperate fear for Ryga's life overrode Kelovin's rational thought. He leaped from his horse to go help Ryga fight. Even getting off the horse caused a severe amount of pain. In the middle of his leap, the pain overwhelmed him. He hit the ground with his body contorting. He screamed out, his vision blurred. He kept trying to move. His eyes were still transfixed on Ryga as he struggled. He found that trying to ignore the pain was impossible. No matter what he did, he could not move past it.

His heart stopped in horror as Ryga fell to the ground, his defenses gone. Visrim spoke with joy, "Your skill was better than most, Elf. You fought with courage. As a reward, I will make your death quick." Ryga's head turned to look exactly where Kelovin was on the ground. His eyes softened and he smiled. Kelovin knew it meant Ryga was admitting defeat. He had nothing left to fight with. He was spending his last couple of seconds to say goodbye.

"No!" Kelovin screamed, pulling himself to his knees. Sweat was pouring down his face; his body quivered. He was in the middle of wrenching himself to his feet when the pain vanished. Ryga's entire body burst into blue flames. Kelovin fell to the ground. He had no more strength to move. Tears were streaming down his cheeks.

Kelovin watched helplessly while another man, similar to Visrim, emerged through the dying flames surrounding them. His hair was colored a tie-dye of sapphire and a dark mud color. The colors of his eyes were a tie-dye of dark blue and brown. He walked as though he was a king. His face was smooth, his cheekbones long. Kelovin let the faces burn into his memory. He swore to himself he would get vengeance upon them for Ryga.

Visrim and his partner continued toward the town they'd passed through earlier. The two of them did not notice Kelovin and Pelmor hiding, protected by Ryga's spells. Kelovin was glad they left; he was unsure how long the spell would continue to hold.

When he was sure they had gone far enough away, Kelovin picked himself up. His legs wobbled beneath his full weight. He pushed the aches out of his mind. One step at a time, he made his way to Ryga's remains. Pelmor stayed behind.

He fell to his knees when he was close to Ryga. The flames had died already, leaving behind only blackened bones and ash. The heat had baked the ground solid around Ryga. Kelovin reached out toward Ryga in tears, "This was all my fault, Ryga. If I had not insisted upon having an adventure, you would still be alive. Why'd you have to command me to remain still? I could have helped you." Anger welled up inside him, followed by an overwhelming grief.

He noticed a symbol drawn in the hardened earth next to Ryga. It was a symbol of hope. It was Ryga's last instruction to him before his death. With tears streaming down his face, Kelovin chipped away at the earth surrounding the symbol with his knife. He hacked at it until he pulled free a chunk of earth surrounding the symbol. He held it in his hands and cried for the rest of the day.

He was still there, the sky now dark, when Pelmor approached. "We must go home, Kelovin," Pelmor's voice was filled with sadness.

"We're not returning to Reshyr until we've found one of the ancient artifacts," Kelovin said without looking up.

"Are you crazy? Ryga is dead. He commanded us to go back. Your oath binds you to do so, or have you forgotten already?" There was no playful tone in Pelmor's voice as he disagreed this time. Pelmor had no intention of pretending he agreed with Kelovin all along after the inevitable fight ended.

"The oath is gone. It is broken by death. I cannot go home right now," Kelovin looked up with fire in his eyes.

Pelmor shoved Kelovin from his knees to the ground, shouting, "You are a child. You're still fantasizing about greatness even after your life-long teacher lies dead in front of you. You did not care for him at all, as you do not care for anyone." Pelmor's words released an anger Kelovin did not know he had. He rose, lashing out at Pelmor, his fist connecting with his friend's jaw.

"Don't you ever say that again," he panted, "Ryga was my teacher. I loved and respected him more than you will ever know. You can leave if you want, I will not." He left out how Pelmor had sat there to watch Ryga die when he, at least, had the power to do something about it.

"Why? Why stay to do something we cannot accomplish by ourselves?" Pelmor demanded.

"Because...if we go home now, it will be as though he died merely because I wanted to selfishly see the world. If I go out and actually find what my father is looking for, then at least it can be said Ryga died helping the Elves rise to greater strength," Kelovin said. Pelmor slumped to the ground, burying his head in his hands.

There was a long silence before Pelmor spoke again, his voice trembling, “I was so scared, I could not even move. I stared and watched as Ryga was killed.” Tears fell from his face. A soft sob escaped from him.

Kelovin’s heart softened as he knelt down next to Pelmor. He spoke softly, “Pelmor there was nothing we could do.”

“Yes, there was. I...I knew Ryga was expecting to die, or, at least, he knew there was a good chance. There wouldn’t have been any other reason for him to release extra magic into our protection spells. He wanted the spell to last past his death. Using so much magic drained him before he even started fighting. I could have come to his aid. I could have done something. I was too scared,” Pelmor’s voice trembled the whole time he spoke. Tears streamed down his face.

“If you had done anything, we would all be dead right now,” Kelovin said. Pelmor continued to cry silently. Kelovin waited. He had cried himself dry hours before.

“Ryga told me I was to protect you. I intend to make good on his wish. I will come with you. We will find this artifact, and afterward, we will tell your father of these renegade Elves to ensure their death.” There was hate in the way Pelmor said *death*. Kelovin did not blame him. He hated them too.

They were silent for a moment. Pelmor looked at Kelovin and asked, “What are you holding in your hands?”

“It was Ryga’s last message to me before he died. I think he was trying to tell me to believe in myself. Hope for the day I will be the great leader everyone needs me to be,” Kelovin said, looking down at the symbol again. They were silent for a while again.

"We should camp here for the night," Kelovin decided. Pelmor nodded agreement. Kelovin carefully put away Ryga's symbol. They unpacked only what was necessary.

Screams turned their attention to the village behind them. Blue flames rose from the houses. Kelovin leaped to his feet as if to go fight them; Pelmor stopped him by holding up his hand.

"It's no use right now. We are not strong enough to stop them. Ryga would not want us to waste our lives after he spent his own to protect them."

He knew Pelmor was right. "Do you know any of the spells Ryga used to protect us?" He asked Pelmor, going back to what he had been doing.

"Yes. I'll put them up," Pelmor said. Kelovin felt the familiar wash of magic come over him, though it did not feel as strong as when Ryga had done it.

"Pelmor, this is the last time I'm going to feel helpless. We must learn from what happened today. We must become stronger." Pelmor clenched his fists, nodding his head. They stared at each other for a moment. Kelovin could see the look of determination in Pelmor's eyes.

Kelovin let his body relax. He lay down, wishing for sleep to take him quickly. His mind did not cooperate with him. When he finally did sleep, it was not well. His dreams were haunted by the two Elves. His mind imagined them in Reshyr—razing it to the ground and killing everyone he knew as he watched. In those nightmares, Visrim came to him last, slowly devouring him with the blue flames.

He woke up screaming. Pelmor, lying next to him, stirred from the noise. Kelovin took several deep breaths. He sat up to have a look around. It was morning. The first rays of the sun were already above the horizon. Behind them, where the village once stood, was only a great black scar upon the ground. Beside him, Pelmor was also waking up.

"It's fruit for breakfast," Pelmor yawned. They dug into their bags to retrieve some breakfast. Kelovin chose a bright orange fruit with a hard, crisp center. It was one of his favorites. "Hey, Kelovin, I realized something," Pelmor said between mouthfuls of his own juicy fruit, some of it dribbling down his chin.

"What?" Kelovin asked him.

"What are we going to do about supplies? You and I held little of our coin and the coin Ryga had on him was ruined by Visrim's blue flames." Pelmor did not look as worried about the prospect as he should have been.

"Well, I guess we are going to have to be smarter about how we use it. No more trading horses. We must only buy food for its actual cost."

"What have you seen to make you believe we can actually do so? You saw what they were like in the last village."

Kelovin thought back to the anger he felt from their flagrant disrespect and obvious overpricing. He realized now how childish he'd been about it. "We'll have to make sure they don't know who we are when we buy things. How much farther is it until we reach the city?"

Pelmor dug into his bag until he found a map. He unrolled it, examining the land closely before answering. "Judging by where we were before, we must be here," he said, putting his finger to a spot Kelovin couldn't see. "So, I would guess we are still about two weeks' travel away or more."

"With enough food, we should be able to make the trip. Once we are there, we will find a way to make more coin."

"Yeah, I bet," Pelmor said. "We'll probably have to eat our horses on the way there and sell our bodies once we've made it.

Some adventure this has turned out to be." Kelovin could not help grinning. The playful tone was back in Pelmor's voice. He knew it must mean he was not as upset anymore about them continuing on, but he was still going to voice his disagreements.

Kelovin decided to have some fun, "You know, you're right. We probably would. I guess we should turn back now."

Pelmor stared at him for a moment in dismay, "You're serious? Well then, I guess I'm ready to go now."

"No, Pelmor, I'm messing with you. We'll be fine on the road. We'll figure things out. Don't worry so much."

He hesitated a moment before chuckling, "I knew you were joking, Kelovin. I was only joking with you. You know how I am. We'll be fine." It was good to know some things would never change with his friend. He rose from the ground. He spoke while packing things up, "I think we'd best start moving. We want to use as much daylight as we can. We'll need to eat lunch on the go and only start dinner close to dark. The more ground we cover, the less food we'll have to buy between here and there."

It did not take long to pick up their camp. They didn't have much. Kelovin mounted his horse. He kicked it into a trot to start across the unbroken plains they'd been traveling through for weeks already. It was a lonelier, more tedious trip without Ryga in front of them leading the way. It didn't help that the scenery never changed much. Thinking of Ryga brought Visrim and his friend's face to his mind's eye. He could still picture them vividly. He would kill them when the chance came. When he was stronger, he would find a way to kill them for what they did.

Pelmor interrupted his thoughts of vengeance with a question, "What do you think your father would say about us doing all this?"

Kelovin thought a moment about it. He quickly decided he did not want to know what his father would say about it.

Whatever it was, it would not be good. "You know, I think he would be happy about everything."

"I was not born yesterday, Kelovin. I know he would not be happy, do you think he would take it out on me for letting you go?" Pelmor asked.

"No. He would know I wouldn't have gone home with you even if you tried to force me. No, I'm sure I would be the one to receive the full force of the punishment. I'll tell him I dragged you along without a choice if you like."

"Yeah, it would be nice if you could," Pelmor grimaced. "I am afraid of your father. Although, maybe it won't even matter. After seeing what happened to Ryga, we probably won't even make it back. He was stronger than us, after all."

"Well, aren't you a ray of sunshine today," Kelovin muttered, tired of all the negativity.

"Sorry," Pelmor grumbled. They fell into a long silence. Pelmor kept his head down, a frown on his face the whole ride. Kelovin suspected Pelmor's pessimism had continued within his head.

When night came, they made their camp in the middle of the plains with nothing around them for as far as the eye could see. Pelmor set to the task of setting up protective spells while Kelovin took care of the dinner.

When Pelmor finished, he took a seat next to Kelovin. Kelovin said, "The protection spells you put up seem to not take much concentration or energy from you. So, why do you think it affected Ryga during the battle?" The question had been poking at him all day.

"The spells I put up are much weaker than the ones Ryga did—a lesser form of them if you will. Those people he fought would have detected us easily if it had been these types of spells. These only protect against regular people."

"That makes sense," Kelovin said, turning his attention to his supper. It was a vegetable soup with a few scraps of meat in it. They did not eat meat often, but it was necessary for their bodies on occasion. Kelovin did not look forward to when their soup would not even have vegetables in it.

When he was finished eating, Kelovin took out Ryga's symbol. Carefully, he chipped away bits of it to create the shape he wanted. While he was working, he thought about the trek ahead of them. It wasn't going to be easy.

Chapter Four

It had been four weeks since the death of Ryga. Travel without him proved to be difficult. With little coin to barter for food, they were forced to buy only when they could manage good deals, which wasn't often. Every village they came to met them with the same hatred. They were forced to conserve what little they did have by eating small portions. The precaution wasn't enough.

They had been out of food for the last week. Kelovin's stomach felt as though it was eating itself from the inside. It was getting harder to keep moving forward. It had taken everything he had in him to get up in the morning and drag Pelmor with him.

The day had already been long by the time the sun had reached its highest point, and now his horse was making it even longer. They had to dismount their horses earlier to give them a rest, which had made his horse happy for some time. Now, hours later, the horse had begun to pull at its reins every chance it got, indicating it wanted to stop. The heat of the sun on top of everything else only put him in a worse mood.

"I think I might see a village up in the distance," Pelmor muttered from beside his own horse. He did not look inclined to trust his eyes until they got closer.

Kelovin peered toward the horizon to see for himself. Sure enough, there was a hazy outline of houses. "I think you might be right," Kelovin said. He did not want to get his hopes up either. They'd been looking for a village for a few days now. His horse tugged at the reins again. Kelovin threw the reins down and turned to his horse, shaking his fist and yelling, "Look, you stupid animal, I'm starving. I don't have an entire field of food sitting in front of me like you do, so we need to find a village. We're all exhausted. The sooner you get moving, the sooner we get to the village and we all rest." He picked the reins back up, wrenching them forward to emphasize his words.

"Yelling at him won't do anything to solve your hunger," Pelmor said. Kelovin's stomach gave a painful groan, as if on cue. He found himself cursing the village behind them once more. The villagers hadn't been willing to sell to them. They claimed some shortage of food. He had wanted to tell them to explain that to his stomach when Pelmor conveyed the news. Unfortunately, there was no persuading them.

"How much coin do we have left?" Kelovin asked, ignoring Pelmor's earlier comment.

"Not much. Even if it is a village up there, we only have enough for a little bit. If we don't reach the city soon and find a way to make more, we might have some problems," Pelmor answered grimly. Kelovin found himself wishing Ryga was there to guide them again. Ryga had been right about one thing. He did miss the safety of the rules as well as Ryga's watching eye constantly protecting them from surrounding dangers.

He reached up, fingering the pendant around his neck. He had coated Ryga's symbol with a mixture of plants and tree sap to strengthen and preserve it. He was grateful Pelmor had paid attention to such things in class. He had fashioned it into a pendant to hang around his neck. It gave him the strength to keep moving on. He shook the depressing the thoughts from his head. Instead, he forced himself to focus his attention on walking forward. No good would come of wishing for the past to change. It would never come true.

"I'm almost sure it's a village," Kelovin commented. The houses had gotten closer and were becoming less hazy.

"Thank the gods. I'm hungry." Pelmor patted his stomach to emphasize his hunger.

"Whose turn is it to go?" Kelovin asked. They took turns every other town because they found their odds of getting food much better when there was only one Elf—on the rare occasion they actually got food.

"It's yours," Pelmor said, pointing at him.

"No, I don't think so," Kelovin said, shaking his head. "The last time, I went. Remember? I got spit in the face by the old man."

"No, I went last time," Pelmor said. "I was persistent, so they tried to assault me. On my way out of the village, they threw apples at me, and I picked them up while I ran."

"You're wrong. That was over a week ago. I remember because it was right before the guard at the next village wouldn't even let me in," Kelovin said.

"Oh, yeah," Pelmor mumbled. A moment later he looked up smiling. "Wait, I remember the last village. They said there was a food shortage. You made me go back and explain how empty our stomachs were. It's your turn," Pelmor said triumphantly. Kelovin sighed. He had been hoping Pelmor wouldn't remember.

"Damn it, horse, I swear I will kill and eat you," Kelovin cursed, shooting a glare backward as the horse pulled at its reins once more. Directing his attention back to Pelmor, he said, "We might as well stop here so we don't get close enough for them to see us. I'll go try and get us some food." He let the horse come to a stop. It immediately went to nibbling the grass in front of it.

"Damned horse," he muttered under his breath as he bent to retrieve a large black cloak from his bag. Putting it on covered any sign he was an Elf. He did not understand why a mysterious stranger was often treated better in the village than an Elf. He tried to forget about it. The need for food was greater than his pride.

"Here's the money. It should be enough to get us a few days' worth of food," Pelmor tossed him their bag of coins. It was not as heavy as he'd hoped it would be.

"All right, I'll be back, hopefully, with food. Set up the spells while I'm gone, just in case." There was no point in taking unnecessary risks. Kelovin pulled the cloak hood over his head as he set off for the village. He left his horse behind. It was important he remain in a good mood in the village, even if it was a pretend good mood, and the horse was definitely not going to help. Traveling to the village by himself gave him a strange fear in his stomach that he could not make go away. He'd gone to villages alone before without incident, yet every time the nauseous feeling came back to him.

Reaching the village took longer than he had anticipated. The sun was already getting low on the horizon, which meant most of the farmers would be getting ready to go home. He hoped that would play to his favor. A farmer who hadn't sold anything all day would be much easier to deal with. They would probably be grateful to get a sale at all before packing up. With his luck, it would probably turn out to be the opposite.

The streets and houses of the village were much the same as all the other ones he'd seen. In the center of the village, he could see several stands with leftover food from the day's sale. Most of the farmers behind them were preparing to go home. The sight of food almost made him run, but he controlled his urge by taking a deep breath.

He passed two stands almost completely empty of food. Those were the farmers who had been selling their products all day; they would only sell at a high price so late in the day. Searching the stands, he spotted one still holding a good amount of food. It appeared to not have had as successful a day as the others.

He approached to see a girl of no more than fifteen years preparing to pack things up. Her sullen face confirmed she had had little luck. No doubt, she would be going back to a disappointed family. "Excuse me," Kelovin said to get her attention.

He got a proper look at her as she turned toward him. Her face was freckled. Her short hair was red like the color of an apple. Her figure was not bad. It looked as though she spent many of her days in the field. "I do not have time for jests. If you're not here to buy food then go away." There was ferocity in her eyes when she said it. He guessed it meant she was not treated well during the day. He did not know much of the human culture. He did know every person he'd seen before had been men, not girls. Perhaps it was not customary for girls to do farm work.

"I want to buy some food. I'm worn from traveling and hungry." Kelovin tried to sound as pitiful as he could to gain her sympathy. He needed to sound desperate. However, not so desperate that he wouldn't leave if cheated. He and Pelmor had honed their skills at obtaining cheap food by collaborating after each of their attempts.

The girl eyed him suspiciously, "I don't sell to strangers I can't see. Take your hood down so I can get a proper look at you."

He shifted uncomfortably. Revealing he was an Elf was a high-risk move. He decided to try to talk his way out of it. "Please, I wear this cloak for a reason. Believe me, you don't want to see what's under here. My money works the same as anyone else's.

Once I have food, I will be gone. It will make no difference to you to see my face." He hoped she would be envisioning some poor ugly wretch beneath the cloak instead of who he really was.

"I suppose you don't want any food then," she said stubbornly, continuing to pack things away. Once one person said no, he knew it would quickly turn to the rest of them saying no as well. Somehow, they always knew he had been rejected, even if he tried to pretend he had left because he had not liked their prices. He sighed irritably and took off his hood, hoping she was the kind of girl who would not care he was an Elf. Her eyes went wide at the sight of his ears, and he knew at once it would not go well.

She turned to run, but he reacted faster than she did. He grabbed her from behind, covering her mouth. He pulled his dagger to her throat. "You will be quiet, or I will slit your throat," he whispered as he pulled her down behind her cart, out of the sight of surrounding farmers. His threat worked. She froze. There was a terrified look in her eyes as tears streamed from them. It almost made him stop the madness he found himself doing. Unfortunately for her, his hunger far outweighed his sympathies.

"I'm sorry I had to do this. I haven't eaten in over a week and need the food. I am going to leave my money here for you. In exchange, you're going to fill my bag with food. Do you understand?" She nodded obediently. "Good. Now I'm going to let you up to gather the food. If you make any move to alert the other farmers, I will kill you." He let her go, and she got shakily to her feet. He hoped she wouldn't take her chances alerting the others. If she did, she would find his threats empty. There was no way he would ever kill her, but what she didn't know was to his advantage.

Her hands trembled with every piece of fruit she picked up. Once it looked like she'd filled his bag with a fair amount of food, he reached his hand out. "All right, good. Now hand me my bag." She handed him the bag while he placed his money on her cart. He had one last thing to do to ensure his escape. "You know Elves have magic, right?" he asked. She slowly nodded. "Good. Then you will know I'm not lying when I tell you this. When I leave, if you make any move to tell someone about me, then I will use my magic to get you." He lifted his hood back over his head.

He forced himself to walk away calmly. His nerves were all on edge by the time he was out of sight of the market. Once he was out of sight, he broke into a run. It would only be a short while before her fear subsided enough to go tell her tale to someone else. He had to be as far away as possible before it happened.

At a full sprint, he was able to return in a quarter of the time it took him to go. He arrived where he had left Pelmor, exhausted. He could not see or hear him, but he could sense the magic when he looked for it. A few moments later, he felt the magic envelop him into its sphere of influence. It was strange to see Pelmor and their horses pop into existence where there had been empty space moments before.

"What happened?" Pelmor asked pacing back and forth, "I saw you running from the village." Kelovin guessed Pelmor probably started pacing the moment he saw him coming back at a dead run.

"Strengthen the spells. There might be people looking for us tonight," Kelovin said between gasps. He still hadn't caught his breath yet.

"What? Why? Did you kill someone?" Pelmor asked, stopping mid-pace to stare at him in disbelief.

"No, nothing so drastic. I only threatened somebody's life," Kelovin said, throwing up his hands. Then he grimaced, "A girl's life."

"What in the blue skies above would possess you to threaten a girl? Don't we have enough problems as it is?" Pelmor was already pacing again. This time, he would shake his head on occasion as well.

"I had to, Pelmor. She wouldn't sell to me otherwise. We have to eat. We don't know how far it will be to the next village. We could starve to death if you like," Kelovin said, clenching his jaw. He did not like being scorned for doing what needed to be done.

"You and I are both good enough hunters we could have gotten our own food," Pelmor declared, raising his voice.

"Look around you, Pelmor. We are in the middle of this god-forsaken plain. Everything can see us coming from a mile away. We've tried before. We would have hunted something already if we were able," Kelovin yelled back.

There was silence for a moment before Pelmor spoke again, "Do you at least have some food?"

"I thought you would never ask," Kelovin said, letting the argument go as quick as it came. He dug into the bag and tossed him a fruit, pulling another one out for himself. The only reason he hadn't eaten something the second he had the food was for fear of being caught by a mob. He felt the magic around them grow stronger while he ate, indicating Pelmor was strengthening the spells surrounding them.

"Get some rest. I will take the first watch tonight," Kelovin said, getting up from the ground. Pelmor only nodded. He was almost asleep before lying completely down. Kelovin marveled at how fast Pelmor always managed to fall asleep. Pelmor's explanation for it hadn't helped at all. He'd said it was like going into a tree except you were giving up your will to sleep instead of to the tree.

A rumbling moan came from his stomach. He ignored it. They did not know when they could get more food, so they had to preserve what little they had. He watched the night grow darker as the sun finished falling below the horizon. The fuzzy outline of the village became lost in the darkness.

He grew restless waiting for the villagers to respond. He even began to think he had been worried for nothing. Maybe, somehow, his threat toward the girl had been effective enough that she would never tell anyone. This thought was quickly extinguished as a line of torches came to life in the distance where he knew the village lay. He waited until the torches had gotten within five minutes of their camp before waking Pelmor.

Pelmor rose in a fright, "Did they find us? Are we being attacked?"

"No. They are coming our way. It's okay. You have your spells up, remember. They won't be able to find us here."

"Maybe they have a wizard among them," Pelmor said stubbornly, but he was not as scared as he was before.

"I did not see anyone who looked to be a wizard while I was in the village," Kelovin said, looking at Pelmor as calmly as he could.

"Yeah, well, your eye to spot things may not be as good as mine," Pelmor said. He had adopted his familiar playful voice again. It made Kelovin smile. It had been a long time since Pelmor had done so.

"My sense for magic is fine. I can spot a wizard if I need to, Pelmor," Kelovin said with a frown.

"Hey, hey, I'm playing with you. I know you can. Don't get so uptight." It was refreshing to go through the farce after so much had happened to them. It reminded Kelovin of his home.

"So, why did you wake me up, then?" Pelmor asked.

"Just in case," Kelovin said. They grew silent as the torches drew closer. Kelovin knew they must be riding horseback with how much ground they were covering.

"We'll let them pass us by, and then I will go to sleep while you keep the watch," Kelovin whispered his words instinctually. It was not necessary because no sound would have escaped their magical walls. Pelmor nodded his approval.

It was strange to watch all of the men pass them by without so much as a glance in their direction. Each man held a torch in one hand, reins in the other. Most boasted some kind of weapon either sheathed, on their horses, or across their backs. Any time one of them would have walked directly into their camp, Pelmor would guide the horses around with gentle nudges from a force shield.

Soon the humans had passed them without incident, so Kelovin went to sleep. His body welcomed it warmly. The next thing he knew, Pelmor was shaking him awake. The world around him was still dark but becoming brighter. When his friend noticed his eyes open, he spoke, "It's early morning. The men never came back this way during the night. I suspect they will be sending some people back this way soon, though. It was too dark to see anything well. They will want to make sure they didn't pass us. I suggest we move now while they are behind us."

Kelovin saw no reason to disapprove of the plan, so he got up to pack his things as quickly as he could. With what little they had it was not hard. "I'm exhausted from the extra spells last night," Pelmor admitted. "I am not sure I would have been able to keep up our protection much longer anyway."

"Well, then, conserve as much energy as you can and eat something. We may have need of your magic still," Kelovin told him. They set their horses off at a trot taking their course well around the village to avoid any wandering eyes. Pelmor was in the lead with Kelovin a few paces behind. He kept checking behind them every so often to ensure they weren't being followed.

His worry receded when the village was far behind them, with no sign of anyone following them. The terrain showed signs of change, however. The plains gave way to a lightly wooded area. The trees did not grow nearly as close together as in Bigor Forest, but there were enough of them to create pleasant shade and homes for woodland creatures.

"We must be getting close now," Kelovin said. "On the map, the city was just beyond the point where the plains ended." It also meant they could forage for more food, a prospect he was sure would liven both of their spirits.

Pelmor grinned, "Looks like we made it. I can't believe after so much journeying we are finally so close." Kelovin wanted to laugh with joy. They knew their journey would become much easier once they reached the city.

"Hey, there they are!" A cry came from behind them. Kelovin looked back to see three men on horses barely visible in the trees. He knew he had to act fast or confront them. He preferred not to kill them.

"Quickly, Pelmor, let's go," Kelovin commanded. If they were going to lose their pursuers, they needed to keep them at a distance. He kicked his horse into a run. Kelovin was glad when it actually ran despite its obvious reluctance. He continued to speak as they rode, "I need you to use your magic to make us invisible but not our horses. Once we're invisible we'll jump off and send the horses in one direction while we go another. If we're lucky, they'll be too far away to notice we aren't actually on the horses anymore." They both worked on getting their bags and weapons untied from the horses while they rode. It wasn't easy while being jostled around.

Once Pelmor was satisfied they had everything, he did as he was instructed with his magic. Kelovin felt it take effect. He rose to a standing position in his saddle and made a grab for a low branch to lift himself from the horse. He was left dangling a few feet in the air. He dropped into a crouch to break his fall. "Pelmor, are you here?" he whispered.

"Yeah." The groan came from some bushes. A second later, the bushes looked like they started shaking by themselves. "My dismount was not as graceful as yours, I'm afraid."

"Come on, no time to waste. We must be gone before they get here." They set off in the direction they had been traveling. Kelovin kept glancing backward until he saw the humans had taken the bait. When they were out of earshot, the Elves ran to ensure their escape.

"Stop!" Kelovin cried out. Pelmor had become visible again without warning. He feared there might be some other wizard nearby. He voiced the concern as Pelmor came to a stop. "Somebody has taken away your invisibility."

"No," Pelmor panted. "No, I ran out of energy to create the magic. I need to conserve what little I have left. I'm not sure I can run much longer either."

"Okay, then let's keep walking. We can eat lunch while we walk." Kelovin had hardly noticed the time passing as they fled. His stomach must have been well aware because it was roaring to be fed. "We can probably eat larger portions this time around. I'm sure we will be able to forage some food here in the woods. We'll do some gathering once we stop for the night or on the way if it's in plain sight."

"Sounds amazing to me, I'm so starved I've almost decided to find out what grass tastes like," Pelmor said. They continued on the path with their eyes on their surroundings. There wasn't as much as Kelovin had hoped to pick from, but some food was better than no food at all.

"I can't believe we don't even have horses anymore. Now we are going to take twice as long to get to the city," Pelmor complained loudly.

Kelovin hushed him. "They could still be looking for us this way, so we can't let anyone hear us." Pelmor's response was to grumble complaints beneath his breath before becoming silent. Their path took a slight uphill climb. They walked all day—straight through dinner—until the woods became dark. They knew the humans could not travel as easily as they could in the darkness, so they stopped for the day. They spent another hour looking for food.

Afterward, they combined their loads to see what they had turned up. Kelovin willed the pile to get larger. It was enough to keep them happy for a day or two. Something wasn't right. There should have been more. He spoke his concern to Pelmor, "It is strange to find so little in a woodland. Usually, there is too much. With this little, I almost feel guilty of depriving the animals of their food source."

"I know what you mean. We need it, though. Perhaps the reason there is so little is because we are so close to the city," Pelmor said.

"There would have to be a ridiculous amount of people living in the city," Kelovin said.

"Well, now that my stomach is settled, I need to rest," Pelmor said. Pelmor was so exhausted he fell asleep the second he sat down. He slowly drifted to a lying position. Not long after, sleep washed over Kelovin as well.

He woke to the sounds of voices. Fear gripped him tightly. Voices meant they would have to fight. He did not wish to kill innocent people just because they thought Elves were evil. He was wondering how it was possible they had caught up to them so easily when he realized the voices were coming from in front of them, getting farther away. "Pelmor, wake up." Kelovin shook him awake. He watched Pelmor's face as his mind went through the same process as his had moments before.

"Who is it?" Pelmor asked, confused.

"I don't know. Whoever it is, I don't think it is the same people chasing us." Kelovin answered.

"Who do you think they are, then?"

"I don't know. Perhaps they are travelers as well, headed in the same direction as us. We must find out where they're headed. Perhaps they are on their way to the city. They could point us to the fastest way there." Kelovin was already packing his things up to go. He slipped on his black cloak in case they were as sensitive about Elves as everyone else. Pelmor did the same.

"What if they aren't friendly?" Pelmor cautioned. His friend no longer shared the same thirst for adventure as he did, Kelovin realized. The fire had been extinguished in him the day Ryga had died. The thought of Ryga saddened him once more. He reached up to touch his pendant, took a deep breath, and pushed it all aside. They set off at a brisk jog.

Before they came into view of whomever the voices belonged to, they slowed to a fast walk. A few more steps got them to the top of a slight rise they'd been climbing since the day before. Down below them was a road. Why it hadn't occurred to Kelovin there would be a road to the city, he did not know. It was only a few feet wide with the occasional underbrush growing in the middle, indicating it was not often traveled. Ahead, there was a small wagon full of barrels and boxes attached to a horse. A man sat upon the wagon, leading the horse down the road. He could not get a good look at him from so far away. Following on foot were a woman and three little kids, presumably his wife and children.

"Let's go ask them some questions," Kelovin said, not waiting for an answer. He heard Pelmor sigh behind him before following. Once they were close enough, he called out, "Hello there."

The man pulled his horse to a stop. He turned to see Kelovin approaching. "Hello," he returned the greeting. Kelovin could see now the man was heavyset. His hair was pulled back in a long black ponytail.

"Might we ask you a couple of questions?" Kelovin asked him. He stopped a few feet away making sure to keep the man's family in his line of sight. No reason to take any unnecessary chances.

"Sure, lad," the man grunted as he hefted himself from the wagon's bench. "The name is Grael." Grael closed the distance between them with his hand extended. Kelovin shook it, then took a step backward. "You might have heard of me before. Grael the Great they call me, Master Merchant of the world."

"I'm afraid I haven't heard of you before," Kelovin admitted.

"No! Well, then this is a special occasion, indeed. It is not every day you run into Grael, you know. I travel all over the world–never in the same spot for more than a few days. I've got things you can only imagine. I can give you a little peek at what I'm bringing in my wagon if you like."

"We need to know if this is the way to the city," Kelovin prompted while the merchant went to his boxes in the back of the wagon.

"The city is ahead. A day's travel, no more. I guarantee you there is nothing in the city you can't find right here with me,"

Grael called back, his head inside one of the large boxes he was digging around in.

"Do you know of a good place to stay while we are there?" Kelovin asked, then added, "A place not too concerned with who is staying there."

"Enough questions until you take a good look at this. This is so much better than a good place to stay." Grael removed a sword from his box. It was long; the blade was slender with runes etched along the blade. "This is a magical sword I picked up while I was traveling among the mountains west of here. Strange lot over there, but they do make good weapons. This sword will never fail you in battle."

"We need to know where we could stay the night. If you don't know, we can ask someone else," Kelovin said, uninterested in the sword. Even if he hadn't known the mountain dwarves would never give one of their precious swords to a human, he would still know the sword was a fake. The runes etched along the side were meaningless nonsense.

"Not a fighter, eh? No worries, I have other wares for you." Grael lumbered back over to his wagon, replacing the sword with a crystal ball. "Now, this is truly unique. Comes straight from the Elves of Bigor Forest, it does. It lets you see any part of the world within its depths." Kelovin could almost not resist laughing. There was no such thing made in Reshyr. With his cloak on, Grael could not see Kelovin was an Elf.

"No, thank you, we must be on our way now," Kelovin told the merchant wearily.

"Wait, I have another product for you I'm sure you won't refuse. Yes, those other two things were trinkets. I've got a real treat for you, especially since you must have been traveling for so long already with no one to comfort you. Woman, come here." The last part he yelled back to where the kids and the woman had been waiting. She obediently walked to his side. Her eyes were trained on the ground the whole time.

Grael grinned, showing his yellow teeth, and put his arm around her. "This, here, is my pleasure slave. Wonderful thing, she is beautiful and completely obedient and has borne me my three wonderful children. There are no slaves like mine. I have more in the city. Surely one of those would interest you." The woman next to him did look as beautiful as he said. She was dressed in rich silks, no doubt to magnify her looks for potential buyers.

The prospect of slavery was not one Kelovin enjoyed, however. He looked at Grael with as cold a glare as he could manage then said, "No, we aren't interested. We must go now."

"Wait, perhaps you can't wait til we reach the city. This is not a problem for Grael. Child, come here." A girl no more than ten walked to his side with her face downwards. "This is Tally or whatever name you would like her to have. I will sell her to you. She is yet young, so she is still a maiden. She is my own blood. I will sell her at a reasonable price." He saw the mother's face tighten in fright.

Kelovin looked at Grael with abhorrence. He had heard there were slaves in other parts of the world, but to be willing to sell your own daughter was appalling. If it weren't for the backlash Kelovin was sure killing him would have caused, he probably would have killed him right then. Instead, he said, "Look, merchant, we have no coin. We are leaving." Kelovin turned and left before any kind of response could be made. If he waited any longer, he wasn't sure his rational side would be able to hold him back. Behind him, he heard the man grumbling something about not having coin. Kelovin paid it no attention.

Pelmor came up beside him and whispered, "If we run, we should be able to get there in no time, especially with this road."

Kelovin looked over at him. Pelmor was practically running already. His feet were moving much more than necessary for the little ground they were covering at a walk.

Part of him said they should be cautious and stay off the road. In truth, he was as anxious as his friend, which is why he said, "Race you there." They both took off at a sprint. The road was, for the most part, unobstructed with only a few obstacles to dodge around. The hood of his cloak was blown off by the wind. He ignored it. He had to concentrate on catching up to Pelmor, who had already pulled a few paces in front of him.

After the first hour of running, their small path connected to a much larger one going in a slightly different direction. Pelmor was still ahead of him and had continued running down the larger path, so Kelovin was forced to follow without confirming it was the right way. Once on the larger road, they passed all kinds of different people. There were people dressed in fancy clothing riding upon strong horses, a group of kids dressed in rags playing as they walked, a carriage drawn by four horses (he could not see who was inside), and many others. They ran past them all, receiving strange looks as they did.

As they were passing another wagon, Kelovin finally pulled out in front of his friend. It gave Pelmor an extra burst of energy. He was beside Kelovin in a heartbeat. Neither of them could talk. All their energy was focused on running. They exchanged a glance. Kelovin could tell Pelmor was determined to win this race. It was strange how childish they could still act after so much had happened.

The road took a slow upwards climb. It did nothing to slow them down. They reached the top at the same time. Both of them nearly fell over as they stopped in surprise. Covering the next hill over, lay the city they'd been looking for. At the top stood a large castle made of stone. It was the most intimidating thing he'd ever set his eyes on. Even from a great distance, it was monstrous.

Spreading around it like a sea was the city. It stretched across the entire hill, even went a little way into the valley between their hill and the city's hill. He thought it was possible the human city was larger than Reshyr itself. It was hard to tell. Reshyr's size was deceptive because it looked like the forest it was in. This city had swallowed the forest hungrily for its buildings. All the trees from where they stood to the city were gone.

"It's impossibly gigantic," Pelmor said in awe.

"I'm glad you can see it too because I was thinking I was starting to see things," Kelovin said.

"It will take us forever to ask everyone about the relic," Pelmor joked.

Kelovin grinned, "Years, maybe."

"Do you want to get a closer look as badly as I do?" Pelmor asked.

"Yeah, let's go," Kelovin said. They both started running again. He was excited to see everything more closely, yet at the same time, he was terrified of the city. He'd never seen anything like it before. They had no idea what to expect when they made it there. They ran until they were forced to slow by the throngs of people traveling the road. There were many of them leaving the city to wherever their destination was, others were making their way to the city with wagons full of things to barter, and still others merely sat beside the road trying their best to get the passers-by to take a look at their wares.

Kelovin pulled his hood back over his head. He noticed Pelmor doing the same thing. There were all kinds of things to draw his attention as they made their way up the road. A small, plump man was selling exotic creatures. He saw a griffin among them. He only knew what it was because of what he had been taught. Other people boasted an assortment of magic swords, armor, furniture, food, and even rocks. The man selling the latter claimed them to be of rare magical material.

The travelers they passed were as interesting as the merchants. There weren't only humans traveling to the city. He'd seen a centaur or two already along with goblins, satyrs, and many other creatures he could not name, though the humans dwarfed their numbers.

It still took them a long day of walking to get through the crowd to the city's entrance. The large walls of the city loomed over them. They were made out of stone. They must have reached a height of forty feet. Its doors were made of wood reinforced with iron. Those doors were large enough to fit twenty men abreast. The sight of it made Kelovin feel all the more overwhelmed, accompanied by a feeling of great curiosity to get a look inside. He tried to move farther, only to find his path blocked. There was some kind of procession ahead of them preventing everyone from going in.

There were hundreds of soldiers lined up in ranks being marched through the gates in an exaggerated show of strength and pride. He had no way of knowing what it all meant, however. He only knew they were causing the delay–keeping him from getting one step closer to finding the relic they sought. They ate their midday meal while they waited for the gates to clear of the soldiers. This time neither of them felt like guessing what they would see inside.

The path cleared as Kelovin was finishing his last bite of bread. He rose triumphantly and said, "All right, let's go in." They walked, hesitant at first, toward the gate. They grew more confident with each step they took. Inside the walls, the city looked even more monstrous. It was hard to see to the top of it where the castle stood. The streets were filthy, teeming with trash, beggars, and more stalls of people trying to sell things. The street ran parallel to the wall in a large circle with streets spaced evenly leading deeper into the city. The buildings were all stacked right next to one another. It made it impossible to go farther in without using one of the streets. All of the rooftops were flat with little nooks. They were perfect spots for archers.

It was clear that if anyone were to breach the city's walls, they would have to deal with archers on their entire approach to the castle on top of the hill. He found himself being moved forward by the flow of the busy streets. Pelmor was still next to him gazing at all of the sights surrounding them. "This is nothing like I've imagined," Pelmor said in disbelief.

"It is like a forest of buildings," Kelovin observed.

"How do we know where to go to ask for information?" Pelmor asked.

"We go to one of those places we've seen in many of the villages–where they sell ale." Kelovin had been pondering upon where they would start asking questions for some time. He had yet to be in one of those buildings. It appeared to him to be the most likely place where many people would be willing to talk.

"Those places seem dangerous, though. And if they're all drunk, then how can we ever trust any information we get from them. I'm not so sure it's a great idea," Pelmor complained.

"They won't all be drunk and it's the only option I've been able to come up with unless you have a better idea."

"No," Pelmor answered glumly. They circled around the street trying their best not to run into people along the way. They had circled half the city looking for an ale-house when they finally came to a building similar to the ones they'd seen in the other villages. A wooden sign hung from the door depicting a wild boar with a glass of ale pouring into its mouth.

Kelovin smiled broadly to Pelmor, "Let's go find ourselves some information."

Chapter Five

The morning's first rays of light gleamed into Kelovin's eyes, signaling morning had come at last. It did not wake him. He would have had to be asleep for it to be able to. He had not gone to sleep the entire night. His mind had been occupied with his regrets.

They'd spent several weeks searching with little luck. It was starting to become depressing. Kelovin was actually thinking about giving up on their quest. The only reason he hadn't was because he did not want to return as the failure responsible for Ryga's death. They had to return with the crystal.

"Are we not dead yet?" Pelmor asked, lying beside him. Pelmor had become less enthusiastic about staying in the city every day. Kelovin was amazed it was even possible for Pelmor's mood to worsen. He already voiced disagreement every chance he got.

"No, we're not. Now get up, there are still many places we have not yet tried," Kelovin said, trying to sound confident. He suspected he did not achieve it as well as he would have liked. He thought back to the day they first arrived in the great human city nearly a whole moon ago. He'd been so sure they would be able to walk into the city and find what they were looking for without delay. Instead, in every tavern they visited, they were turned away, scorned by those they sought information from, for both their race and their lack of coin.

Kelovin reflected on the first tavern they'd gone into called the drunken boar. They'd entered the building with high spirits. The smell inside was worse than the city. It was poorly lit, creating a gloomy feel. The tavern was mostly empty, except for the owner and a few silent, drunken patrons.

He had walked up to the owner confidently and asked, "Where can we find information on the ancient god relics?"

The owner looked him up and down for a moment before responding with a hearty laugh, "What does a filthy Elf want with the god artifacts? Your kind is not acknowledged by the gods, they will do you no good."

"What we want with them is our business. We just need to know where to seek them out," Kelovin said.

"Information like that is going to cost you," the owner said.

Kelovin knew they did not have much money left to barter with for information, but it was important they complete their quest. He pulled one of the smaller coins from his bag and put it on the counter. "Tell us what you know," Kelovin said.

The man picked up the coin and inspected it. "This won't get you much," he said, holding out his other hand for more.

"That is all we have to offer," Kelovin said.

"Then the best I can tell you is you might have some luck talking to the drunkards in here. Sometimes they are willing to give out information."

"If you will not provide us information, then kindly return our money," Kelovin said, trying to remain as calm as he could.

"I did give you information, which means this is mine. Now, get out of my sight before I get real angry and call the guard, filthy Elf," the owner said, turning from them.

Kelovin didn't see any other option, so he turned away from the counter and walked toward one of the patrons. Once he was close enough to be heard without speaking loudly he asked, "Excuse me, sir, can we ask you for some information?"

The patron looked up from his drink and snarled. He spoke as loud as he could, "I'm not to talking to no pointy-eared freak." The rest of patrons in the tavern burst into laughter.

Kelovin felt Pelmor's hand on his shoulder as he whispered, "Come on, Kelovin, we aren't going to get any help here." Kelovin had nodded his agreement, and they'd left the tavern to search somewhere else.

After the first tavern, they had begun systematically searching the city for others. Information did not come cheap–as they had soon found out—except for useless information. They were given all kinds of free information they couldn't use, even without them asking for it. They had found out, from one of the drunken men they had talked to, that the city was called Eaglepoint. The man informed them it had gotten its name when it first started as a strategic fort for the defense of the kingdom. It was one of the highest points around the area, so people approaching from any direction could easily be seen.

When the king had made the fort his home, it became the city Kelovin and Pelmor had entered. The commoners called it Crow's Nest because of all the rotting things within the city. The Elves had listened to the drunkard patiently because he was one of the only ones to give them any information at all. When they pressed about what they wanted to know, the man had cursed them out the door.

Over their days within Eaglepoint, they had covered over half of it. They were no closer to the information they sought. To make it worse, they had no way of buying food. In order to eat, they either had to make money or make the trip back to the forest to forage. A trip to the forest meant spending one day to get there and find food, then most of the next day to get back into the city.

Kelovin hated wasting so much time. He would not allow the trip unless they were desperate. Pelmor's question earlier was an indication he felt it was time to make the trip. It had been three days since their last meal. Kelovin reached up to clutch his pendant of hope. He found himself wishing once more that Ryga was still there to help them. The wish came more frequently over the last couple of days as their situation became more hopeless.

He could not let Pelmor know how defeated he felt, so he rose from the ground they were sleeping on. They were outside the city gates. It was no use trying to sleep within. The guards would not allow it. Heading back into the city, he saw the gate was already busy with people trying to get through, as it almost always was. They had learned it was one of the greatest trading cities in the land. Some claimed you could find whatever you desired there, no matter how obscure the object—not without coin, though.

"Do we have any of the berries left to eat?" Pelmor asked. He rubbed his stomach as his eyes pleaded for the answer to be yes.

"No, we ate the last of it three days ago," Kelovin sighed, his head slumping downwards.

"My stomach is killing me. We need to find food today, not worry about asking for information."

"You're right." Kelovin's own stomach was hurting so much he could hardly think. He tried telling his stomach he had gone longer without food before, but it wouldn't listen. They had no other option except to find food.

"I am?" Pelmor asked. He was not used to Kelovin agreeing with his complaints.

"Yes, today we will focus all our time on finding someone who will trade work for some coin so we can buy food."

"We've tried working already. No one will hire us. We need to scavenge for our food," Pelmor argued. He was right. Every time they had sought out work, they were always turned away for the mere fact they weren't human. No one would hire them without, at least, seeing their faces first, either. It was compelling to spend the day hunting for food instead. However, Kelovin refused to waste two whole days. He knew they could figure out how to get hired somehow.

"No, we aren't going to waste more time than is necessary. We've wasted so much time already. We will find a way to get hired and buy our food. If you want to eat, start thinking of clever ways to convince people they want to work with us," Kelovin said, holding out his hand to help Pelmor up from the ground. Pelmor took it, hoisting himself up.

"We should go home," Pelmor said, as he had hundreds of times before.

"No," Kelovin declared hotly. "I will not abandon our quest. All we need to do is try harder."

"This folly will be the death of us," Pelmor grumbled.

"If you want to go home, then leave," Kelovin turned away toward the city gates, kicking a stick in his path as hard as he could. Pelmor followed behind him despite his protests. Once past the gates, they made their way toward the third circular street. There were twenty of the streets in all. Each became smaller as they progressed up the hill. The buildings on the higher circular streets echoed the compactness of the first street, which only allowed passage through certain side streets. The higher areas had fewer side streets to gain access to the next circle. They had found out quickly that the higher they went, the less popular they were.

The third circle was full of mercenaries looking for work. Workers would gather there each morning. Those who needed help came to choose from the people standing there. When they discovered it, they had tried going the first time with their faces hidden. It was then they had discovered it was impossible to get work with their identities hidden. They had to stand there all day after everyone had come and gone before someone told them. Even after they were told, the chances of getting work were not good. The number of people who came seeking work far outweighed the number of people hiring.

The lack of employers was caused by the many factions that existed within the city. They all had their own mercenaries for all sorts of work. The factions were trusted. Only the reject mercenaries the factions refused to accept came to the street for hire, which made them the last choice among mercenaries.

That day, however, when they arrived, there were only a few people there before them. The appearance of the few who were there looked as desperate as Kelovin felt. They did not have to stand there long before a well-dressed man walked up, announcing he had need of them all. Kelovin and Pelmor exchanged a look of joy. They had not expected to get work at all, let alone so quickly.

The man led them through the streets higher up the hill, talking as he went, "As you know, the Lords' feast is tonight. My lord sent me to hire a few extra guards for the night, as he does not think his guard is sufficient. He may be right. People tend to get crazy at the Lords' feast."

"What's the Lords' feast?" Kelovin asked, his curiosity piqued.

"I will not explain myself to a filthy Elf. You're lucky I was desperate enough to allow you to help." Kelovin knew better than to make any comment back, so he resigned his curiosity to following the man. They wound their way up to the fifteenth street where all of the lesser lords and rich commoners lived.

They were led inside a white house. The room they came into was large with a high ceiling. The floors were made of a dark green marble. The walls and end tables were all barren, as though everything from the room had been removed. The man leading them motioned to a few seats. He said, "Your task will be to break up any fights starting out among the commoners. You will wait here until the feasting starts." The man turned through another doorway, leaving them to wait.

A man slightly older than they were turned his attention to them. There was nothing remarkably out of the ordinary about his appearance. He spoke softly, as though someone might hit him for talking, "The Lords' feast happens once every year. It is the rich folks' way of thanking the poor folk for protecting them in a time of need. This city was once threatened by an overwhelming attack. Thousands of the poor folk gave their lives protecting the city. The king proclaimed a feast in their honor. The feast has been upheld every year since. All of the rich folk open up their homes so the poor folk can come from the lower streets to partake of the feast put on by each individual house."

"Then why would there be fighting at such an event?" Pelmor asked.

"With so many poor folk in one area with free alcohol at their disposal, there are bound to be disagreements," the man said, grinning.

"Why are you talking to the likes of them?" an older man with a large gut growled in their direction.

"You can keep to yourself. Leave me and my choices alone," he responded.

"Whatever, Elf-lover," the older man said, though he still appeared disgruntled. It was obvious he did not wish to start any fight at the risk of losing his job. Kelovin would never understand the deep-seated hatred the human race held against them. The Elves had never wronged them throughout all of history. If anyone should be hated, it should be the humans. They were the ones who betrayed all the other races at one time.

The man who hired them continued to come periodically throughout the day to give them more instructions on what they should do. Kelovin and Pelmor were given posts where they were least likely to be seen. It had the added benefit of making them the least likely ones there to have to stop any fights. They were also given explicit instructions to hide their faces at all times. The owner of the house did not want others to know he had stooped to hiring elves for his house's protection.

Night came eventually. With it came the poor and hungry. Kelovin was amazed by what he saw. The house filled to the bursting point shortly after the doors were open to the public. Everyone was either stuffing as much food as they could in their mouths or draining more alcohol than should have been possible. Kelovin was guarding a stairway, in a remote part of the house far away from the food and wine, ensuring no one went upstairs. Pelmor was down the hallway preventing people from entering guest bedrooms.

With everyone's focus on the other side of the house, Kelovin became bored. His stomach growled constantly with the smell of food so close. He still didn't dare leave his post to sneak some food. They would get their pay soon anyway. Afterward, they would be able to buy themselves plenty of food, more than for one night. No one had come within five feet of him since the festival began. He was leaning against the wall counting the numerous self-portraits the owner displayed when a drunken man stumbled toward him.

He stood straight, speaking as slow and clear as he could, "I'm sorry, sir, this area is off limits. Please return the way you came."

The man stared up at him with his eyebrows furled as if he was trying to work something out. "I jusss...wan-ta...go shlep," he managed to slur. Before Kelovin could respond, the man stumbled into him with his hands grasping for some kind of hold to keep from falling. His fingers clenched around Kelovin's hood, jerking it off as the man righted himself. Kelovin caught hold of him and moved him back toward the main part of the party. The man cried out in surprise, "Itssss an Elf."

Kelovin took a couple of small steps backward. A good portion of the room had turned to see what was going on. The drunkard fumbled in his clothes until he found a hidden knife. "I'll teesh you...toushin me." He was only able to take a few steps forward before Pelmor threw a knife into his head.

The room erupted into panicking people yelling for the guards. Kelovin turned on Pelmor, yelling above all the chaos, "Why did you kill him?"

"He was threatening you. I'm supposed to protect you," Pelmor shrugged his shoulders.

"This isn't like at home, Pelmor. There are consequences for the way we handle things. You didn't even think before you killed him, did you?" Even as he spoke, several guards were pouring into the house, struggling against the wave of people. "We'd better get out of here," Kelovin said, motioning for Pelmor to follow him out the back. They'd only gone a few steps when the other hired hands blocked their way.

Pelmor strode forward, pulling his sword out. Three against one wouldn't be an easy fight, even if Pelmor was a superior bladesman to them all. A look behind them did nothing for Kelovin's optimism. There were already half a dozen armed guards closing in behind them. The hairs on the back of his neck rose. He had to do something fast, or he and Pelmor were going to die. Steel rang as Kelovin released his sword from its scabbard. He leaped forward, swinging sideways with all the strength he could muster. His intentions were to knock the three hired hands' blades aside so they could run past. Instead, as his blade met each of theirs, it shattered each one into pieces, including his own on the last impact. The room around them went silent. Everyone, including himself, stared at the broken swords strewn about on the floor.

Those precious seconds wasted robbed them of their escape as more guards arrived in the back, blocking their path. With their arrival, the others already present snapped back to reality. They advanced toward the Elves once again.

"When I say 'run,' do it. Don't think about it," a voice from directly behind Kelovin whispered. No one had been there a second ago. Kelovin's head snapped around to see a small Elf with lemon-yellow hair wink at him. Kelovin assumed he could trust another Elf offering help, so he nodded agreement. "Okay, run!" the Elf yelled out, charging forward straight toward the guards. He felt they were surely running straight to their deaths. Since they were going to die anyway, Kelovin followed the Elf with Pelmor right behind him.

Screams erupted from the crowd. Gale force winds shoved the people in front of them to either side, throwing many of them off their feet. Yet, somehow, the three of them remained unaffected. It was an impressive display of magical control, especially since there was very little nature to draw the magic from. There wasn't much living within the city aside from humans and animals. It had limited Pelmor from using magic the entire time they were within Eaglepoint.

Their rescuer did not slow down as he led them, weaving through the crowds of people strewn about. They passed faces full of shock and fright by the hundreds. They would have drowned in the sea of people had it not been for the wind forcing people out of their way. Kelovin's footsteps rang out against the stone roads, signaling they had escaped the crowded areas. The Elf dropped his magic wind and continued to guide them through the streets, zigzagging back and forth to the outer rings of the city.

"Where are you taking us?" Pelmor called out ahead of them.

"Somewhere safe," the Elf yelled back.

"How do we know it's safe to be with you?" Pelmor shouted back.

The Elf stopped running. He turned back toward them. Once they caught up he said, "What do you mean *you*? How do I know I'm safe with you," he grinned from ear to ear. "After all, I'm the one who risked everything to save you–complete strangers—from certain death."

"He has a point, Pelmor," Kelovin glared at him before turning to the Elf. "I'm sorry for my friend's ungratefulness. His name is Pelmor, and my name is Kelovin, the Prince of Elves. We are grateful for your help."

"Haha. And I'm the bloody king of the universe," the Elf threw his head back, laughing.

"You don't recognize me? I am the true prince..." Kelovin began, unsure what to say.

"Kelovin!" Pelmor hissed. "You remember what Ryga said about revealing your true identity."

"Yes, I remember. I hardly think he was talking about other Elves when he warned us about it," Kelovin said.

"He could be a renegade or something. It was other Elves who killed Ryga, after all," Pelmor said. Pelmor's words made Kelovin tense up. His jaw clenched as Visrim's face came clearly to his mind's eye. Their rescuer was left to stare back and forth between the two of them.

"You truly are the Prince of the Elves? But how is it possible if you are a Defra? I thought most Elves did not even know of our existence," Miko said.

"A what?" Kelovin asked.

The Elf stared at him even longer, tapping his finger against the hilt of a knife at his side. Kelovin noticed Pelmor watching the knife while shifting uncomfortably. The Elf must have become aware of it too because he waved it off saying, "We have no time for this at the moment. We must be on our way. For now, all you need to know is my name is Miko, and I am going to help you." Miko turned back down the street. Kelovin followed. He knew if he did, Pelmor would follow as well.

After winding through the streets for a couple of hours they came to a house in the fourth circle of the city. "This is it," Miko said, leading them inside, "Are you two hungry?"

Kelovin and Pelmor looked at each other, their stomachs simultaneously answering for them. "Yes, we haven't eaten for days," Kelovin echoed his stomach.

Miko chuckled, "What is a prince doing without coin in a human city?" He retrieved some thick soup from a simmering kettle as he spoke, "Burgor always leaves some food prepared for me to eat when I get home. You two can eat as much as you want."

"Who is Burgor?" Kelovin asked.

"The man who lets me stay here. I will have to talk to him in the morning about you two staying with us for a few days. Most likely, you will have to help us with work, though," Miko said.

"We have no problem working," Kelovin said between mouthfuls of soup, "We've been trying to work for food this whole time anyway."

"Great, there will be time for more chatting tomorrow. I'm off to bed. You two finish eating, then get some sleep. The floor will have to do for now. I promise you will be safe here, and don't worry, there will be more to eat tomorrow," Miko gave them a wink with one last chuckle before disappearing.

Once he was gone, Pelmor threw up the protective enchantments to hide them from sight and block their noise from others. Kelovin shot him a quizzical look. "We still don't know them. We especially don't know how this Burgor is going to react if he finds us here," Pelmor explained. "I say we count our blessings and take off before morning, perhaps taking a little extra food since he's already offered it."

"No, absolutely not, even if he hadn't already saved our lives," Kelovin held up his hand to stop Pelmor's protest. "He did save our lives. So, even if he hadn't done so and hadn't given us food, there is still much I want to learn from him. I have questions I need answered. Besides, he may have a way to get us the information we need to continue our quest. Like it or not, we need to stay here, Pelmor."

"Fine, but we stay hidden within these spells until we can determine Burgor is not going to be a threat to us," Pelmor folded his arms, glaring at Kelovin.

"Have it your way, but it won't be necessary." Kelovin rose from his seat, setting his empty bowl next to the empty pot. Picking a spot he figured to be out of the way of normal foot traffic, Kelovin laid down to sleep. "We can't suspect everyone of being evil, Pelmor. Not everyone is." Kelovin closed his eyes. Sleep did not come as easily as he hoped.

He thought about Pelmor. It was clear their journey had already changed him significantly. He was no longer optimistic about anything. He hardly ever bothered covering up his disagreements the way he used to, either. The latter wouldn't be so bad if he didn't disagree with everything.

He did not remember when he finally fell asleep, but he must have as he woke with Pelmor nestled close to him. Noise was coming from the fireplace. He sat up, shaking Pelmor awake as well. At the fireplace, he saw a large human. The apron he wore was covered in blood. Standing next to him was a little girl humming a song Kelovin did not know.

Miko walked into the room. The little girl squealed, throwing her arms around Miko. Miko looked over her head, straight at them, and winked. "How does he see us, I thought you put up the protection magic?" Kelovin asked.

"He can probably sense the magic. I was not capable of putting up strong ones last night. We hadn't eaten for days, after all," Pelmor said.

Kelovin turned his attention back to Miko who was talking, "Burgor, I need you to remain calm and trust me for a few minutes. Can you do it as favor for me?"

Burgor grunted, "What have you done this time Miko, eaten all the bread?"

"No," Miko beckoned to the Elves, "I have a couple of guests."

Pelmor dropped his magic, revealing them standing in the corner of the room. Burgor rose to his full height. He was actually an intimidating man. The butcher's knife in his right hand only made it worse. "Who are these men, hiding in my house like rats?" Burgor roared.

The little girl yelled, "Awesome, show me how to become invisible too." She stared up at Miko waiting for an answer.

Miko ignored her to address Burgor. "Well, they are Elves, actually. My friends. They only hid because you're so scary, Burgor. I mean, look at you. You're the size of a mountain," Miko gave him a playful shove with a small gust of wind.

Burgor visibly relaxed, but only a little. "Who are you?" he asked.

"My name is Kelovin and this is my friend Pelmor. We are out on a journey given to us by our king," Kelovin said.

"They were down on their luck, about to be murdered, so I helped them out. I was hoping you would let them stay here for a couple of days to get back on their feet," Miko said.

"Only if they can contribute," Burgor growled.

"I'll take them hunting with me today. I'm sure they will prove to be super helpful," Miko said.

"If you say so," he muttered, waving his hand. He turned back to his pot.

"Come along then, you two," Miko said, "There is a ton of work to be done. We're behind already. I've taken the initiative to pack us some breakfast." Miko detached the little girl from himself. "You have to stay here, little one. This mission is for big people," he said. The girl kicked the floor. She shuffled back to her father's side, dragging her feet the whole way.

Miko led them out of the house, toward the city gates. Kelovin caught up to Miko and began to speak, but Miko interrupted him by raising a hand to stop him from talking. Miko had them continue on in silence until they had retrieved a cart and horse from some stable and left the city behind them.

When they had trekked the distance to the forest's edge on the east side of the city, Miko turned to them, "I know we both have many questions for each other. I wanted to get well away from the city before we started openly discussing things. Too many hidden ears reside within the city. Out here we don't have to worry."

"You said something about Defra last night. What are they?" Kelovin asked.

"Uhhh, they are your kind, although you seem to be ignorant of the fact. Well, the history behind Defra is a lengthy explanation, so I won't go into it right now. I can assure you, you are no regular Elf. You are a Defra Elf," Miko said.

"What do you mean? How do you know? It can't even be possible. What are Defra anyway?" Kelovin spoke rapidly, not even sure himself where he wanted to begin.

"I will explain it all, don't worry. First, I want you to answer my questions," Miko said, folding his arms.

"Kelovin, I must reiterate, we don't know him well enough to put all of our trust in him. Let's go our separate way, we don't need him," Pelmor said, glaring at Miko.

"We have no choice, Pelmor, we need his help," Kelovin said, turning back to Miko, "What are your questions?"

"Are you truly a prince of the Elves?" Miko asked.

"Yes," Kelovin said.

"For how long?" Miko asked.

"All my life. Why would it be any different?" Kelovin asked, his forehead wrinkling.

"And you have no previous knowledge about being a Defra Elf?" Miko asked.

"I don't even know what Defra Elves are. Never heard of them," Kelovin said.

"Then what are you doing out here?" Miko asked.

"My father has sent us on a journey to retrieve one of the four great artifacts," Kelovin answered.

"With only the two of you? No offense, but I don't think a king would send the two of you at your skill levels on a journey like this, especially if you are his son," Miko said.

"He also sent my mentor Ryga with us. He was murdered some weeks ago. We encountered someone much stronger than we could have anticipated," Kelovin chose to leave out the part where their adventure was supposed to have been a farce the entire time. The thought of Ryga made him instinctively reach up for his pendant.

"What did you just touch?" Miko said pointing at his chest.

"It is something my mentor left behind for me," Kelovin said. He showed it to Miko.

"Good enough, for now. First, you most certainly are a Defra Elf. I am sure by now you have discovered your magic does not work like the other Elves," Miko said.

"I have not been able to use any magic since birth," Kelovin admitted, hanging his head.

"No, there you are wrong. You did magic last night when you broke those three blades with one swing. You think you can do something so crazy normally? You must think pretty highly of yourself," Miko said. Pelmor snorted.

"How? What do you mean?" Kelovin asked, shooting a glare back at Pelmor.

"I guess the easiest way to explain it is to tell you about our magic. Each Defra Elf is born with a special magic. Each kind of magic controls a specific aspect of the things you see all around us. It is easy to tell who has what power because both our eyes and our hair reflect those powers. You having gold hair and eyes means your magic is concentrated around strength. Last night you used magic to enhance your strength in order to break those blades," Miko explained.

"Can Defra have more than one type of magic?" Pelmor asked.

"Yes, some have several, in fact," Miko said.

Kelovin and Pelmor looked at each other at the same time, the same thought occurring to them simultaneously. Kelovin was the first to voice it, "Those Elves who killed Ryga were Defra Elves."

"I told you we shouldn't be trusting this person," Pelmor spat angrily.

"Whoa, now. Not all Defra Elves are created equal here," Miko said smiling. "After all, you found your prince here is one as well."

"Why would an Elf kill another of his own kind? I thought Elves were supposed to be a peaceful race?" Kelovin asked.

"Well, if your kind would not hide your history, you would know all of this already. The magic Defra Elves carry is greatly influenced by their emotions. Depending upon their magic, they have specific, special bonds with certain emotions as well. Unfortunately, there is one whose bond is with hatred. The Elf in question has an uncanny knack for spreading his hatred into others, which has created a society of Defra who are willing to kill for the fun of it."

"Then why are you not the same?" Pelmor asked, folding his arms.

"Well, we all have the choice of what path we are going to follow. I chose not to follow the evil path, being evil isn't my kind of thing. Besides, the opposite side exists as well. It always does. There is a chosen one whose bond lies with charity, or pure love, if you will. She too has a great influence over others."

"So there is a division among the Defra?" Kelovin asked.

"Exactly. It has been escalating into a war no other race sees coming because all of the intelligent races have simply forgotten our existence. Unfortunately, this war will affect everyone. There are some Defra who hold extraordinary powers and could cause major havoc on the land," Miko said.

"This all seems a bit much to be believable," Pelmor said.

"Well, it is to you because you've never heard of all this. It is like second nature to me because I grew up with it. It is all we are taught from the moment we are born; prepare for the impending war," Miko said.

"If this is all true, we must go tell your father, Kelovin," Pelmor said.

"If this is all true, then it means it is more important than ever we go find the artifact. You saw what two of those Defra could do. Imagine an army coming toward us. We are a people who have not seen battle in thousands of years. We would be slaughtered. We need to gain some advantage," Kelovin said.

"We don't even know what these artifacts are capable of or if they will even do anything at all. Let's go home, Kelovin," Pelmor pleaded.

"No. We can't go home, not yet," Kelovin turned away from him to make it clear he would not discuss it any further. He spoke to Miko once again, "Can you train me how to use my magic?"

Miko smiled, "I would certainly be happy to."

"Can we start now, then?" Kelovin asked. Pelmor sighed, throwing his arms up in the air. He stomped away a short distance.

"In a few moments. First, we need to go hunt before all the good stuff gets caught," Miko said, getting into a crouched position. "You guys up for a race?"

"Seriously, he is childish. Kelovin, we don't need him," Pelmor complained, having to speak loud to be heard from where he was.

"Not long ago, we were doing the same thing, Pelmor. We most definitely need him," Kelovin said. He turned back to Miko again, "We've tried hunting before. We've never been able to find anything. Usually, all we find is fruit and such."

"You guys didn't know where to look. There are specific spots where there is still a decent amount of things to hunt. Usually, it's the more dangerous areas. Nothing we can't handle," Miko said.

"How far do we have to go?" Kelovin asked.

"A couple miles south of here should do. Are you ready?" Miko asked. When they both nodded their heads, he shouted, "Ready, steady, go!" All three of them took off. Kelovin and Pelmor found themselves blown down by a sudden gust of wind. Kelovin jumped back to his feet, pursuing him as fast as he could. He didn't bother to see if Pelmor had done the same.

Miko was going impossibly fast and his own progress was impossibly slow. Minutes later, he saw Pelmor sprinting past him. Evidently, Pelmor had figured something out he could not, as Pelmor was now going almost twice as fast as Kelovin was. Then it came to him. He realized Miko must have been creating a backwind of some sort to slow them down. Pelmor must have figured it out sooner and created a force shield to divert the wind. Frustrated at his own lack of ability, Kelovin veered off to the right to get out of the stream of wind.

Both of them had already gained too much distance on Kelovin for there to be a chance of catching up. From what Kelovin could see, despite Pelmor's best efforts, Miko was running faster than him.

Miko stopped after four miles were behind them. He stood waiting for them to catch up. "Looks like I'm the fastest one here," he said when they finally did.

"Only because you did not give a fair contest," Pelmor growled. There was sweat streaming down his face.

"No one said magic wasn't allowed. Now, if you two don't mind, help me find some meat to bring back to Burgor. Once we've got a good amount, we can begin your lesson." The three of them split up, spending a few hours hunting. Between the three of them, they were able to get over a hundred pounds of meat. "This should make Burgor happy," Miko declared. "Now, let's get started."

"You said all Elves have an emotion attached to their magic. What is mine, then?" Kelovin asked.

"Yours is fear," Miko said.

"Fear?" Kelovin asked. He hadn't been expecting such an emotion.

"Yes, fear. It is more complicated than you imagine. It does not necessarily have to be something obvious, like the fear of dying. It could be something as simple as fearing you might lose something important to you or the fear of failure," Miko explained.

"So, all Kelovin has to do is become the biggest coward the world has ever seen, and he will become strong," Pelmor scoffed. "This is idiocy."

"No, the emotion does not dictate completely an Elf's capability. It only enhances or decreases one's power. Magic is much the same as any other muscle in your body. The more you use it, the stronger it becomes. This is why Elves are superior with magic to most humans. They live longer, therefore, they have developed their magic longer. We have discovered that Defra tend to exhibit unnatural amounts of the emotion attached to their power. Time allows you to control its power over you," Miko said.

"So, how do I use this magic?" Kelovin asked.

"Tomorrow," Miko said holding up a hand. "It's late already. I need my beauty sleep. I will show you how to use your magic before going back to the city."

"All right," Kelovin sighed. He had waited this long to use magic, one more night wasn't going to kill him. Kelovin looked at Pelmor. He had a look saying he wanted to disagree with the decision, so Kelovin spoke before he could voice it. "Pelmor, can you put up our protection spells? We'll be spending the night here. We can't pass up the opportunity for me to learn how to use magic."

Pelmor stood stationary while he decided whether or not to push the matter. In the end, he nodded and went to work putting up the spells.

"These spells are pretty awesome. I wish I could do something similar," Miko said. He lay on the ground, "I'll see you folks in the morning." Miko closed his eyes.

Kelovin looked at Pelmor and shrugged. Kelovin lay down as well. His mind was racing with all the information he'd been given. It took a while before he was able to force himself asleep.

The next morning, when Kelovin woke up, Miko was already up with breakfast ready to eat. Pelmor was already eating. "I didn't think you guys would mind a little breakfast," Miko said, handing him a bowl of dried fruit and meat.

Kelovin accepted the bowl, "Thank you."

"Can we get back to explaining to Kelovin about his magic so we can be on our way?" Pelmor said.

Kelovin shot Pelmor a glare, then said to Miko, "Don't pay him any heed, but I would like to learn more about it."

"I suppose I would be anxious to learn if I were in your position. Well, as you know, Elvin magic is normally used from the elements surrounding us. For the Defra it comes from inside," Miko began before being interrupted by Pelmor.

"You mean chaotic magic. Like the humans use. Kelovin, using chaotic magic is not worth the consequences," Pelmor said.

"No, it's not the same. There is a special connection to magic within us, not present in any other species. It is what gives us the capability of performing great magical feats normally not possible to others. The only drawback is our magic is limited to only specific things. Then again, you are only limited within your element by your own imagination. So, Kelovin, I assume you have the ability to sense magic and have practiced doing so," Miko said.

"Yeah," Kelovin muttered remembering the countless hours of struggle to do any kind of magic.

"You have been taught where to find the magic humans use from within themselves?" Miko asked.

"Yeah," Kelovin said. He'd thought about tapping into it before, despite the side effects. Cutting down his life span would be okay with him if he could do magic. It was the reasoning he'd given to his father in an attempt to convince him to allow Kelovin's use of chaotic magic. It was strictly forbidden. It was one rule he never broke. His father told him there was more risk than harming one's own health, many other things could go wrong as well.

"Okay, then concentrate on it. Let me know when you've focused on it," Miko said. Pelmor was about to say something until Kelovin shot him a glare, shaking his head.

Kelovin took a deep breath. He let his senses open up to the magical currents surrounding them, then he went inward to his own. Chaotic magic got its name from the great risk a person ran using it. You never could be absolutely certain what would happen when tapping into your own life source. The humans did it because they could not access the magic in the nature surrounding them as the Elves could.

"Okay, I've found it," Kelovin said.

"All right, now you need to look deeper. You will find a magic source that feels different than the one you feel now," Miko instructed.

Kelovin did as he was instructed. For several moments he could only feel the same thing. It made him fear he would fail at this lesson like all of the others. The thought made him try even harder. He would do this or pass out from exhaustion before he quit. Then what he was searching for lit up like a beacon to his mind's eye. The magic source felt strangely familiar to him, as though he'd been using it his whole life. Trying to remain calm and focused, Kelovin said, "I've found it."

"I'll admit I can feel the different source too. How can we know this magic is not as dangerous as chaotic magic?" Pelmor interjected. It was possible for experienced people to sense magic streams in others, but not possible for them to use those streams without a battle of wills between two.

"You're going to have to trust the guy who knows Defra history on this one. We have been tapping into this magic for thousands of years to no consequence," Miko said.

"Pelmor, please. If this works, then my whole life will make sense. Don't you want me to discover more about myself?" Kelovin said.

Pelmor sighed. Sitting down, he said, "Yes, I also want to make sure you're still around after all this as well. You're still my best friend."

"Okay, good. Now, let's continue," Miko said. "As I have said before, your magic is concentrated on strength, so we're going to start with a simple exercise." Miko walked up to a tree. "I want you to focus on using your magic source to send strength through your arm. There are two ways to do this. The safe..." Miko was saying.

"No, tell me the most powerful way to do it," Kelovin demanded, interrupting him.

"All right. In order to do it, you must focus the magic into your shoulder. Then I want you to punch the tree. As you punch, send the magic coursing through your arm to your fist. It is important you time it right because your magic's strength also protects your body from harming itself. This method will give you the greatest force for the least amount of magic," Miko said.

"Does it have to be a living tree we practice on?" Kelovin asked.

"Huh? Why?" Miko asked.

"Trees are pretty important back where we live. I would rather not harm one for my own benefit," Kelovin said.

"All right, I suppose I can find a dead tree somewhere if it will make you happy," Miko said.

"Yes, I would be more comfortable." Kelovin smiled thankfully. Miko closed his eyes. Streams of air formed going in all directions from where Miko stood.

He opened his eyes, "All right, this way." He led them a quarter of a mile from where they were to an enormous fallen tree. It could not have fallen more than a few days ago, as it had not rotted much.

"How did you find this?" Kelovin asked.

"I can feel the wind as I direct it, so I sent it out and found a spot where its travel was impeded by a log. It takes a little finesse and concentration. No big deal. I will welcome all praise given," Miko said, flourishing with a bow.

"You blow the wind real good, now can we get back to teaching Kelovin? The sooner you do, the sooner we can be rid of you," Pelmor said.

"All right grumpy pants, relax. Kelovin, do as I said before with your magic, then punch the log," Miko said.

Kelovin walked up to the log. He could feel the magic well up in his shoulder as he concentrated. He raised his arm to punch when Miko called out, “Wait. You’d better use the other arm first.”

“Why?” Kelovin asked.

“Trust me on this one,” Miko said. Kelovin started the whole process over with his left arm instead. The current of magic moved down his arm as he swung. Then his world was sent into spinning chaos as pain reverberated through his body. He felt bones in his hand break in a few different places.

Pelmor was at his side, “Let me see your arm, I can help.” His vision was so cloudy he could not see Pelmor take his arm. Pain left him as quickly as it had come. His vision cleared. Elvin magic was restricted in its ability to heal wounds because the energy cost was too steep, but it could allow the body to ignore pain. Thankfully, Pelmor could easily use magic to set his bones back in place so they could heal properly too.

“Why would you let him hurt himself?” Pelmor turned toward Miko, already gathering magic.

Kelovin caught his arm, “No, Pelmor. It’s not his fault. I chose not to use the safe method.”

“He could have warned you,” Pelmor said.

“I would have ignored the warning,” Kelovin said.

“Well, at least I made you use your other arm,” Miko’s smiling face came into view. “Look at what you did.” Kelovin looked at the log he punched. Half the trunk’s diameter had been knocked to splinters, scattering the area around it. Kelovin gasped. “And this happened with your swing being interrupted by a timing issue. I told you it was important to time it right. This is why. Are you ready for the safe method now?” Kelovin nodded his head. “All right, this time instead of concentrating the magic to one spot, I want you to send it through your entire arm at the same time and then punch."

Kelovin slowly got up. "You're going to do it again? Are you crazy?" Pelmor asked.

"Don't worry, if he does it this way, he will be protected. Nothing bad will happen," Miko said. Kelovin turned to the log, positioning himself where it was the thickest. He estimated it to be between two and three feet thick. He concentrated his magic to his shoulder once more. He was behind his entire life in learning magic. He was not about to learn any slower than he had to. He swung again. This time his timing was perfect.

Kelovin fell to his knees as his fist went through the entire tree, continuing partly into the ground. Splinters exploded everywhere. Both Pelmor and Miko stared blankly at the destruction. "You did that with your magic concentrated in your entire arm?" Miko asked.

"No," Kelovin smiled. "I tried the first way again."

"You're crazy," Pelmor said.

"How fantastic. I like a person who's willing to take risks. It is an impressive amount of power for not having realized you even held this kind of magic before. Now, there are many things you can do to begin learning more control and accuracy. You don't want to be some big brute whose sole purpose is to hit hard, after all."

Miko bent down to pick up a rock, "Obviously, my magic is not the same as yours, so there is only so much I can do for you. I know some of the exercises others have done to improve their strength. For example, take this rock." Kelovin grabbed the rock from his hand. "Now close your fist around it." Kelovin did so. "Good, you're going to squeeze it, trying split it cleanly in half. If you master the correct application of strength, it should come out perfectly smooth on both sides of the rock. Don't ask me how because I don't know. I only know it's possible. Now give it a try."

Kelovin concentrated his magic to his hand and squeezed. When he opened his fist, powder sprinkled from his hand. Miko laughed, "Still need to work on it, I think. Another thing you'll need to make sure to work on is conditioning your heart and lungs. You may be able to make it so your limbs never tire, but you still have to breathe. Don't worry, your magic will help you as well. You should have enough to get you started. Also, one last thing, Strength Defra tend to be fairly good at recovery. If you send a constant small stream of magic toward your broken bones, they will heal faster and stronger than they normally would."

"You have been helpful. We are in your debt," Kelovin said.

"Well, if you guys help me haul the meat back, you should be able to stay one more night at the house and have some supper. Wouldn't want you two to starve," Miko said.

"Okay," Kelovin said.

The trip home took much longer carrying the meat with them. Once inside the door, Miko called out, "Burgor, I have some tasty meat for you."

Burgor emerged from the kitchen. His eyes fell on the large pile of meat behind them. He opened his arms wide saying, "My friends, what a great bounty you have brought home with you today. You are most welcome to stay for a little while. This should be enough to keep putting food on the table a bit longer."

"Thank you, Burgor. Your hospitality is appreciated. We'll try to stay out of your way while we're here," Kelovin said.

"Nonsense. Friends of Miko are no bother," Burgor said.

"Come on. Let's go see what's cooking," Miko said, walking into the kitchen. Kelovin felt the weight of the last few weeks fall off his shoulders. Things were finally working out for them.

Chapter Six

Kelovin woke up before sunrise the next morning in a good mood. He was the happiest he could ever remember being. The things Miko taught him the day before had answered many questions about himself he'd yearned to know all his life. He finally was not a failure. The problem with all the answers given was they created more questions he hadn't had before. Who were his real parents? Why hadn't they raised him themselves? These were only some of the questions he now had. He doubted Miko would know the answers.

Pelmor woke up next to Kelovin. He sat up, rubbing his eyes awake. "I don't know how you ever managed to sleep without a tree. I'm never going to get used to it. It's so exhausting. Not hard to fall asleep, but hard to get good sleep," Pelmor said.

Kelovin laughed then clamped his hand over his mouth. "I almost forgot others are sleeping here," he whispered.

"Don't worry, I'll put up a sound block," Pelmor said. The air around them shifted slightly, infusing with magic. Pelmor continued to talk, "Since you've learned what you wanted to, I think we should leave here and head back home. We've accomplished something, so Ryga's death won't be in vain. It is important for your father to know of the impending war and the existence of the Defra Elves."

"I know you want to go home, Pelmor. I can't explain to you why, but I feel I have to do this. It's almost like I'm being pulled further along. Can you please hang in there with me for a little while longer?"

Pelmor sighed, "Fine, you are the prince, after all. Can we at least ditch this Miko guy?"

"What is your problem with him? He has helped us so much already. He's done nothing to upset you as far as I can tell," Kelovin said.

"I don't trust him. I can tell he's a reckless kind of person. He has the ability to convince everyone around him to be reckless. I don't want him to get us killed."

"What a ridiculous assessment. Have you even been conscious these last few days? He's the one who saved us. Are you even the least bit excited I've finally learned I can use magic? Or how about how I've discovered I haven't been defective my whole life? He's the one who made it all possible," Kelovin said.

"Forget I said anything. Yes, I'm happy for you. It's actually pretty incredible," Pelmor said.

"I've only scraped the surface of who I am, there are so many more questions to find answers to. I don't even know where to begin," Kelovin said.

Miko entered the room, cutting off their conversation. When he saw them up he said, "Oh, good, both of you are up already. I took the liberty of packing us as many supplies as we can carry. I got us some horses as well. I hope you don't mind, I invited myself onto your journey. I think I can be of great help to you."

Pelmor released the magic blocking their voices. He said, "We don't even know where we're going."

"I do. I did some poking around with the help of my friend Burgor," Miko said, giving them a wide grin.

"Amazing, we've been trying to get information for ages. How did you do it so easily? Where do we need to go?" Kelovin asked, jumping to his feet.

"I will tell you as long as I hear agreement that I can accompany you," Miko said.

"It would be our pleas..." Kelovin said.

"No," Pelmor said at the same time.

Kelovin sighed, turning to Pelmor, "After all this time spent killing ourselves for information on where to go next, we finally have some at our fingertips. You want to turn this opportunity down?" Kelovin asked.

Kelovin couldn't believe Pelmor actually sat silently debating his answer. "I suppose not, you can come with us," Pelmor relented.

Miko smiled. He said, "Good, I was hoping you would see reason. I am an enjoyable companion, after all. We're going to travel northwest of here to pay a visit to the Wizards' Guild. They should be able to lead us in the right direction. After all, they have an artifact of their own."

"Great, at least now we have somewhere to start," Kelovin said.

"Fair warning, the wizards aren't a polite and sociable kind of folk. We're definitely going to have to work to get information out of them." Miko gave Pelmor a wink, "Nothing we can't handle."

"Well, let's get going then." Pelmor huffed, grabbing his things, then heading for the door.

"That's the spirit, Pelmor. We'll be there in no time," Miko said.

"Don't talk to me," Pelmor responded without looking back.

"Don't worry about Pelmor, he'll come around. He always does eventually," Kelovin said as he patted Miko's shoulder.

"I'm not worried. No one can resist my charm forever," Miko said. They shared a grin before the two of them followed Pelmor out the door. As they made their way to the north gate, Kelovin bent down to pick up a few dozen rocks, placing most of them in his pockets. He carefully closed his fist around one. He squeezed, visualizing what he wanted to happen. He frowned as dust spilled between his fingers. This was going to take longer than he thought.

"Don't worry, you'll get it eventually," Miko said. Kelovin nodded. He pulled the next rock out of his pocket. Repetition was the only way he was going to learn. The rest of their trek to the gate passed in silence. Pelmor led the way. Once outside the gate, Pelmor was unsure where to go, so Miko had to take over the lead. Pelmor moved to the back, grunting complaints under his breath.

They traveled for an hour without incident, each one lost in his own world of thoughts. "Yes!" Kelovin broke the silence, causing both Miko and Pelmor to jump.

"What are you hollering about?" Pelmor asked, going to Kelovin's side.

"My rock isn't dust like all the others. See? Look," Kelovin held out his palm. Inside was a rock split into four different-sized pieces.

Pelmor grunted, picking up a piece of the rock, "It doesn't look like a clean cut down the middle to me. Next time you don't accomplish your goal, please refrain from giving me a heart attack."

"It's not right but definitely an improvement," Miko observed. "You are making remarkable progress. You must have been using magic your whole life without knowing it to be able to keep doing this exercise for so long."

"I don't know what you mean," Kelovin squinted his eyes at Miko.

Pelmor laughed, then said, "As usual, Kelovin, you never did pay attention to any lessons you were given growing up, did you? We were taught that magic is like any other muscle. In order to do more and make better magic, you first have to build up your magic endurance. Otherwise, your body can't handle it. I assume it is the same for Defra, although their magic is different."

"Pelmor is right. The amount of magic you've done so far should have made you pass out from fatigue long ago. You must have been subconsciously using magic to make yourself stronger your whole life without knowing you were doing it," Miko said.

"See, you should have listened to me growing up. I told you to pay more attention to our instructors," Pelmor gloated.

"Well, I don't see how any of the information is useful to me anyway. Unless knowing I should be out of energy is going to somehow help me break the rock the right way." Kelovin said, folding his arms.

"No, but it is something you must keep in mind in the future. Crushing small rocks is no large task. Therefore, it does not run any high risk. On the other hand, if during a battle you're already exhausted from fighting and you decide to try something ridiculous you've never done before, let's say, picking up a six-ton boulder to throw at someone's head, it's possible you could push your body over the limits and kill yourself," Miko explained.

"All right, I get it. Enough school lessons now. I've had plenty of them my whole life," Kelovin said.

"There are countless miles of road in front of us. We need to get going, anyway," Pelmor said. The usual silence returned to their trek.

It wasn't long before Kelovin's mind wandered. It was strange how different Eaglepoint was from his home. The inhabitants of Eaglepoint devoured the natural resources around them while punishing those who weren't lucky enough to get any, whereas, his homeland was comparable in size, and their surrounding resources only continued to flourish. No Elf was ever cast down to live in poverty. So far, the human race had proved to be something he did not prefer to be around.

Kelovin was lost in his thoughts until he realized the horses had stopped. Miko was talking. "This should be a good place to stop for the night. We are only a couple of hours away from the wizard community."

"If we are only a couple of hours away from it, then why don't we press onward?" Pelmor asked.

"Because it is dangerous at night. They have many traps laid for nighttime intruders. The morning is much more sensible," Miko said.

"Great, I'm exhausted anyway," Kelovin said, dropping his stuff to the ground.

"Fine, I'll put up our protection then," Pelmor said. Pelmor started his usual routine, muttering to himself as he cast the magical barrier surrounding them.

"Don't forget to include Miko into it," Kelovin said. He figured Pelmor had shown enough dislike for Miko that he needed to make sure.

"I'm sure he can protect himself," Pelmor said.

"Pelmor, come on," Kelovin said.

"Fine," Pelmor huffed. He continued to grumble under his breath.

Kelovin watched Pelmor. He couldn't help smiling. Pelmor was as loyal a friend as anyone could ask for. Pelmor had never left his side in all his life. "Ow," Kelovin grimaced as a twig hit his head, interrupting his thoughts.

"Sorry, air current," Miko muttered. Kelovin looked around to see dozens of twigs and branches flying as if by their own accord to where Miko stood. He ducked as another branch nearly smashed into him.

"This time it was on purpose," Miko laughed.

"How do you know where to direct your magic if you can't see all of them?" Kelovin asked.

"I can use the air to see beyond my sight, remember?" Miko said, shaking his head. He added, “You really don’t pay attention when learning things.”

Kelovin ignored the comment. "You can register all of it at once?" Kelovin asked.

"I’ve gotten pretty good at it over time. For me, it’s basically the same as actually seeing everything with my eyes,” Miko said.

"Wow," Kelovin said.

"Our magic can do much more than it appears. It is only restricted by your own imagination and ability," Miko said.

Pelmor walked up, finished with the protection spell. He asked, "Can you light those sticks on fire?"

"No," Miko said.

"I guess you are limited then," Pelmor said.

"Pelmor..." Kelovin began.

"No, it's a fair point," Miko interrupted. "The thing is, even though I don’t know how doesn't mean there isn't someone out there smarter than me who would be able to figure it out. The point is, you shouldn’t let yourself get stuck in only doing the obvious when using your magic. You must explore and experiment every chance you get to unlock your true potential."

"What's for supper? I'm starving," Pelmor changed the subject.

"I was thinking some soup would be nice," Miko said.

"Wasn't asking you," Pelmor said.

"Right, silly me," Miko laughed. "So, what will it be, Kelovin?"

"Soup sounds fine," Kelovin shrugged his shoulders. He sat on the ground, putting his head in his hands. He was tired of Pelmor constantly attacking Miko. He was more afraid Miko might eventually grow tired of it as well. If he left them, it meant the end of discovering more about his past. Everything he tried to ease Pelmor's mind failed. He couldn't figure out how to stop Pelmor's dislike for the Elf.

He picked up a rock, twirling it in his fingers, mulling the problem over. Dwelling on his difficulties only left him despairing about the future. While he sat in his misery, he felt his magic source surge with extra power. It leaked into him without him commanding it to. The magic's strength cleared his mind. He looked down at the rock he was twirling. A new idea came to him.

He closed his hand around the rock, visualizing a line going through his hand and the rock, straight down the middle. He felt the magical strength pooling in the imaginary line. He continued concentrating until the line was paper-thin and was the only place he could sense the strength. Kelovin slightly squeezed his hand together, making sure to keep his focus on the line.

Slowly, he let his eyes open to stare down at his now open hand. There was his rock split cleanly in half. Kelovin jumped to his feet, "Pelmor, Miko, look!"

Pelmor leaped to his feet, weapon in hand, looking every direction at once. "What is it, Kelovin? What do you see?"

Miko immediately sent out a wave of air to detect any intruders. "I can't find anything unusual," he said.

"No, there's nothing wrong," Kelovin laughed. "Come look at this rock." He grinned widely as he presented his rock to both of them.

Miko laughed, "You've done it. Remarkable."

"I was sitting over there thinking when I felt this strange wave of strength flow through me. The power made it easier to concentrate on what I had to do," Kelovin said.

"It's an amazing accomplishment," Pelmor smiled. "Next time, try to be a little less alarming when you tell us something."

"So, what were you scared of?" Miko asked.

"What do you mean?" Kelovin thought Miko must be able to read his mind.

"Our powers are connected to emotions, remember? When we feel an emotion connected to our power, it is amplified. So, you must have been thinking of something you feared," Miko said. Kelovin had not completely understood what Miko meant the first time he told him. It made more sense now.

Kelovin was silent for a moment. "I was thinking about what would happen if I lost any more of my friends on this adventure. I've already lost so much," Kelovin said. It wasn't the complete truth. He figured it was enough of the truth to explain what happened.

He felt Pelmor put a hand on his shoulder, "Don't worry. I'll make sure it doesn't happen anymore."

"Fear is not always a bad thing. As long as you control your fears, you can use them to provide strength you wouldn't otherwise have." Miko said.

"All right then, I'll get back to making dinner, shall I?" Pelmor smiled, "Seeing how Kelovin has figured out the first lesson, perhaps you should give him the next thing to work on."

"You're right. The next one they usually taught in my village continues your ability to focus your strength in precise measures. You will be using rocks again for this exercise. This time, instead of splitting them in half, you will be squeezing them to make a perfect circular sphere. You have to be able to crush or break off all the pieces of the rock that are keeping it from having the shape you want," Miko explained.

"I'll have to start working on doing it tomorrow," Kelovin yawned. "Right now, I'm exhausted. I want to get food in me and promptly go to sleep afterward." Pelmor nodded and got to work on cooking.

The rest of the evening was quiet. Sleep came easily to all three of them. The next morning, Kelovin woke up in a peaceful mood. He saw both Pelmor and Miko were already up eating breakfast. "How long have you been up? Did you even sleep?" Kelovin asked.

"We haven't been up long," Pelmor said.

"You woke at the perfect time. We barely finished making breakfast," Miko said, handing Kelovin some food. Once the food was in his hands, Kelovin found he was extremely hungry. He gulped his food down as fast as he could. The hunger must have been the result of his training the day before.

"Let's get going. I'm anxious to learn more about this artifact we're searching for," Kelovin said.

"I am too," Pelmor agreed.

"Well, then, let's go. It isn't far now. We'll probably be able to see it once we get over the next hill," Miko said, jumping to his feet. The three of them packed up their belongings, setting off again for the wizards' tower.

Miko was right about it coming into sight over the next hill. Kelovin got to the top to see their path went down into a deep valley. Towering out from the bottom was the largest castle he'd ever seen. Admittedly, he'd only ever seen one other one. He had a feeling this one was irregularly large anyway. The bottom of it almost engulfed the entire valley floor. The top of it was nearly at eye level from where he stood, though it was several hundred feet to the bottom of the valley.

"These wizards have always liked to overcompensate. Their castle is far larger than they need. They like to intimidate people," Miko said.

"Well, it's working," Pelmor said with his mouth gaping open. "How did they ever find the time and materials to construct such a place?"

"It's something they've been adding to ever since it was first established, mostly through magical means. They've occasionally added some parts through physical construction when they could afford to. They've put in nearly the same amount of effort into traps activated during the night to prevent anyone from descending into the valley without their knowledge."

"I almost feel like I can jump onto the castle from here," Kelovin said, still astonished by its sheer immensity.

"Well, I don't recommend it. The jump is much farther than it looks, anyway, we won't get anything accomplished sitting here. Let's go introduce ourselves, shall we?" Miko said beckoning them to follow him.

"Are we sure these people like visitors?" Pelmor whispered to Kelovin as they followed Miko down into the valley.

"Their castle is big enough to have visitors, besides, you can't miss it," Kelovin shrugged.

"Having a big castle doesn't tell us they're the kind of people who take kindly to visitors," Pelmor said.

"Wizards are selfish. They also hate outsiders," Miko called back. Noticing Pelmor's surprised look, he added, "I can control the air carrying sound around me. I always intensify the amount I can hear to be aware of anyone trying to surprise us. Consequently, I can hear you even when you are talking softly."

“You seem to have an endless number of tricks going on at the same time. How do you have so much access to magic?” Pelmor asked.

“My younger years were not hospitable times. I had to constantly get stronger with magic to survive. I guess there were some positives to being raised in hell,” Miko said. His yellow hair’s vibrant color faded to a darker mustard color.

Kelovin could see Miko did not like discussing his past, so he changed the subject, "If wizards are not the friendly sort, then what makes you think they want to help us?"

"Because wizards are also greedy. For the right price they tend to forget how selfish and unfriendly they are," Miko said.

"We don't have anything we can possibly offer them," Pelmor said.

"I'm sure they will think of something. It’s not often they have three powerful elves stroll in looking for some answers. They will make a deal," Miko said.

"What makes you so certain?" Pelmor asked.

"I just know. Now, stop your bickering and come on. This will get us far closer to obtaining your artifact than anything you’ve done up to this point," Miko smiled. He took off running down the hill yelling back, "Come on, I'll race you there."

Kelovin looked at Pelmor. He was surprised to find there were no signs of him being upset. Pelmor looked back at him saying, "Let's go." Kelovin stared after him a moment as he took off running. He did not understand the change in his attitude, but he was not going to complain. Kelovin took off running, trying to catch up to the other two. By the time he caught up, they had arrived at the front door of the wizards’ towering castle.

From the valley floor, the structure was even more impressive. All of its walls were intricately designed. Its immensity filled Kelovin’s entire field of vision. The door in front of them was fifty feet tall with swirling symbols painted all over it. At the top of the door were two large circular openings. Each was about the size of two of his fists. Beneath the circles, an inscription was written. It read, *If you wish to enter, blow down the doors.*

"What do you think it means?" Pelmor asked.

"It means we need to figure out how to let ourselves in," Miko said with his eyes fixed on the door.

Kelovin walked up to the door to push on it. It didn't even budge a little bit. He felt something weird beneath his hand as he pushed. "Hey look here, this door has handholds on it. I think it's supposed to go down, not in." Kelovin gripped the handholds, pulling down as hard as he could, pouring his magical strength into it. The door wasn't going anywhere.

"Hold up," Miko said, raising his hand. "I think there is something else we must do first." Miko sent a wave of air into the circles at the top of the door. Within them, he could feel heavy locks holding the door in place. The release mechanism was within the circles as well. Miko sent a heavier blast of air into them causing the locks to be released. "Now pull," he said.

Kelovin concentrated as much strength into his arms as he could and pulled again. The door slowly slid down into the ground. There were more handholds above the first ones to allow him to keep pulling downwards. Once the door was halfway down, all the resistance gave out. The door slammed the rest of the way down, almost pulling Kelovin's arms with it.

The door opened into a hall large enough to comfortably fit a house. Standing a few feet away was a man dressed in loose clothing. "We've been awaiting your arrival," he said. "Come right this way, please. The Mystic Lord would like to speak with you." Miko snorted. The man's eyebrows creased downward before he turned around to lead the way.

Kelovin and Pelmor looked at Miko for direction. Miko shrugged, following the man. Pelmor and Kelovin followed right behind him. They were led all the way across the great hall. Traversing the entire length took what felt like forever. Kelovin found himself wondering why anyone would want to live in such a large place. There was so much unnecessary space. To him, it was a waste of resources and an insult to nature. Despite the fact he would never dare build something so atrocious, he had to admit the results were impressive.

The man stopped in front of a door that was constantly changing colors. "How is it changing colors?" Kelovin asked.

The man grinned, "A gift from the dwarves. This door is magically designed to open into any room in the castle. We could have done it ourselves, but we like to give others the chance to make themselves useful in return for our vast knowledge."

"Yeah, I'm sure your concern for others is always what governs your actions. Your overwhelmingly humble need to help others is astonishing," Miko rolled his eyes, chuckling.

"I would watch what you say when you are in our household," the man scowled.

"Please, all we want is to meet with whoever is in charge here." Kelovin stepped forward before Miko could make any reply.

"Follow me," the man said. He swung open the door, revealing a lavishly decorated room with a large purple crystal at its focal point. Kelovin immediately felt an unnatural pull toward the crystal. He took a few steps forward to see it better. There were white swirls intricately running over the entire surface. The crystal itself appeared to be alive. Although it was stationary, it gave the appearance of continuously shifting. There was definitely a huge source of magic emanating from it, but it was unlike any other magic source he had ever felt. The magic was immense. Kelovin was tempted to reach his will out to the magic source.

"We are proud the gods deemed us worthy to hold such an artifact," a voice from deep within the chamber said. "You can feel its power, can't you?"

Kelovin pushed down his urge to try and interact with the crystal. "Yes, it's extraordinary," Kelovin found himself saying.

A tall man, elegantly dressed, walked into view, "Allow me to introduce myself. I am the Mystic Lord Raizen." Miko snorted again. Pelmor elbowed him in the ribs to quiet him down.

Kelovin shook his head to try to block the crystal from his thoughts, "My name is Kelovin. These are my companions, Miko and Pelmor. We have come here seeking your knowledge."

"I see, it is not often we get Elves coming here seeking for our guidance." From the corner of his eye, Kelovin could see Miko whisper something to Pelmor. Pelmor fought back a chuckle. He returned his focus to Raizen who was still talking, "Why do the Elves seek to do so now? I can assume you have come from your home city on official business from the king, can I not?" Raizen asked, turning his head to the side slightly.

Kelovin was about to answer when Pelmor stepped forward, speaking before Kelovin could. "You can't assume anything. We are on our own quest right now. Not everything we do must go through the king."

"Right, right. There was not offense intended, my friend. So why are you here, then?" Raizen asked.

"We are looking for another of the lost artifacts. Seeing as you have one, we thought you could give us some direction on where we might start looking for one," Pelmor said.

Raizen grinned, "Yes, these are extraordinary, aren't they? We've had this one for some time. I'm afraid it's been so long since we last searched, it would be difficult to give a good answer, but I do believe we can be of some assistance if you are willing to do us a favor first."

"What kind of favor?" Miko asked, stepping up as well.

"There is an extremely rare herb we want. The trouble is, you can only find them within the Traveling Forest. The good news is the forest happens to be nearby to the north at the moment. Unfortunately, we can't spare the time to go get the herbs ourselves. If you would be willing to retrieve us some, we will exchange information with you," Raizen said.

"One moment please," Miko smiled at Raizen. He then turned to Pelmor, nodding to him while motioning to his ears. Pelmor raised a sound barrier around them. "They could probably break the magic if they wanted to," Pelmor said. "There isn't a ton of energy to draw from in here."

"Are you sure? I feel like there is a stronger amount than usual right now," Kelovin said. He saw Miko nod to himself, as if in agreement. It was strange Pelmor felt nothing. To Kelovin there was an overwhelming amount of magic swirling around them. It was part of what was distracting him so much.

"Look around you, Kelovin, there is no nature to draw from," Pelmor said.

"They won't risk being discovered and coming off as rude. They are trying to convince us they are nice," Miko said to get back on subject. "We can talk freely."

"What is the traveling forest?" Kelovin asked.

"It's a dangerous place, full of Defra who don't care about anyone outside their forest," Miko said.

"Can we trust the wizards? If we do what they want, will they give us the information we need?" Kelovin asked.

"Doubtful. We must find some way to force them to share what they have," Miko said.

"How did you plan on getting them to tell us in the first place?" Pelmor asked.

"I don't know. I thought we'd figure it out once we got here," Miko laughed a little.

"I thought you said you had a plan. What are we going to do now? This whole thing was pointless," Pelmor threw his hands up, motioning to their surroundings.

"I have an idea I think might work," Kelovin said, "especially if they are willing to take playing nice further than they already have. Let me talk to them."

"All right, let's do it then," Miko said, nodding to Pelmor again. Pelmor dropped their sound barrier as they all turned toward Raizen.

Kelovin stepped forward this time to speak. "We find your terms agreeable, as long as you're willing to perform a blood oath. My companions here do not feel you are worthy to take part in such a ceremony; however, I believe you to be a man of honor. So long as you do not divulge its secrets, we will do the blood oath. Then we shall complete your task."

Raizen grinned, "The Elvin blood oath. I must admit, despite having heard a lot about it I have never actually been able to see what one is like. I would like to have the experience once."

Kelovin stared in disbelief. Pelmor leaned in and whispered, "How does he know about blood oaths? Elves don't ever mingle with humans enough for him to know about it." Pelmor's words voiced the same thoughts he was having at the moment.

Raizen's grin somehow grew larger, "You thought I was ignorant of the oath and sought to use it against me. Come now, my friends, you don't honestly think we've become the central location of knowledge without picking up a few things here and there, do you? Don't fear. I will choose to ignore the offense. I have nothing to hide. I would be happy to agree to the blood oath."

"We meant no offense," Miko said, stepping forward when Kelovin could not think of how to respond. "We must admit, we are surprised you know of the blood oath, but there is no desire to trick you. We only must guarantee the trouble we go to for you will be justly rewarded."

"Of course," Raizen said. His voice remained as pleasant as he had begun, but his eyes betrayed his true feelings. There was anger in his eyes. "How do we perform this blood oath?" Raizen asked.

"We need to be in an area with trees," Kelovin said, having regained his composure.

"Easily rectified, follow me," Raizen said, going toward the door they came in.

As they walked, Kelovin could feel Pelmor throw up another sound barrier before asking, "Why would he agree to the blood oath if he knows what it is? Didn't you just tell us the wizards will never hold up their side of the agreement?"

"I don't really know what the blood oath is, but whatever it is, Raizen probably thinks it will not be able to hold him to his word," Miko said.

"Do you think he could actually find a way to break a blood oath?" Kelovin asked, looking at Pelmor.

"I doubt it," Pelmor said. "The wizards do seem to be stronger than I thought, but no one has ever been able to break a blood oath before."

Pelmor released the barrier as they approached the door. When Raizen opened it, Kelovin paused. He saw a large courtyard in front of them.

Raizen smiled, "As you can see, the door works from both sides." Raizen strode into the courtyard toward several ancient-looking trees, "Will these work for this purpose?"

"Yes, these will do fine," Kelovin said. "Stand in the middle of the trees. Pelmor will stand next to you to walk you through your part while I do the other."

Raizen walked to the middle of the trees, "Now what?"

"We'll need you to prick your finger to draw some blood. The blood is extremely symbolic in the oath," Kelovin instructed.

"Okay," Raizen complied. Looking at Pelmor, who had walked up to one of the trees surrounding them and placed a hand on its trunk, he asked, "What is he doing with the trees over there?"

"Pelmor is asking the trees to be a witness to our ceremony," Kelovin said. Pelmor exerted his magic to help the trees move into a perfect circle.

“Impressive magic,” Raizen said.

“Our ancestors emphasized symbology greatly. The trees represent nature’s circle of life,” Kelovin explained.

Pelmor turned around and said, "Okay, we're ready." Kelovin stretched his hand out. Raizen took it. As soon as he did, Pelmor made the trees send vines out enveloping their arms. Raizen jumped in surprise. Yet, somehow, he still managed to retain his cool demeanor.

Pelmor stood next to Raizen and softly spoke the words Raizen was required to say. Raizen repeated the words with exactness, "I, Raizen Klome, make this oath by the blood of my body, binding my body and soul to the oath I shall speak. I covenant I will provide any information I can in regards to the crystal Kelovin seeks when the herbs requested are brought to me. I will not let any human wizard within my power kill or harm

Kelovin or his companions." Pelmor stopped speaking and looked at Kelovin.

Kelovin could feel Pelmor's magic mixing with the trees surrounding them to finish the oath. Kelovin spoke the finishing part, "I seal this oath created by Raizen, receiving his blood." As the vines turned red, Kelovin could feel Raizen try to jerk his hand backward as he felt the powerful magic take hold of him. It was too late. The vines would not let go until the oath was over. Kelovin continued, "And I declare if this oath shall be broken, he shall feel unbearable pain unto death until he intends to obey the oath."

The vines disintegrated, turning to ash. Raizen snatched his hand back, rubbing it before regaining his composure. "We have a deal, then. I trust this is enough to satisfy you. This is the herb you'll be searching for." Raizen made a magical picture of what the herb looked like.

"Yes, we will be back with your herbs soon," Kelovin said. "Thank you for participating in our tradition." Kelovin turned back toward the magical door, bringing the exit from the castle to his mind. When he opened it, he was gratified to find the exit on the other side of the door. Miko and Pelmor followed him out.

Once they had gone some distance away, Miko asked, "Will the oath actually work?"

"Far better than Raizen realizes," Pelmor said. "I've never met anyone who has been able to break a blood oath without dying before. It's been among the Elves for thousands of years."

"That was brilliant, then," Miko laughed, "He probably thinks his magic can undo whatever magic he just let take hold of him."

"I could tell by his reaction he did not expect the magic to be as powerful as it was, but now we have to get those herbs, otherwise it won't matter," Kelovin said.

"I'm sure it will be no problem. I'll lead the way. From what Raizen said, it actually isn't far from here." Miko took off at a brisk jog toward the north end of valley with Pelmor and Kelovin close behind. The hill on the north side was a gradual climb.

Miko stopped at the top. He said, "See? It's right over there." Kelovin reached the top and looked out toward the horizon. The hill went down for several feet then leveled out into a flat, grassy area. Half a mile in front of them was the start of a forest.

"Why did Raizen call it the Traveling Forest?" Kelovin asked.

"Because it moves. In a couple of months, it won't be in this area anymore," Miko said. "The Defra who live there are powerful Defra with control over vegetation. They're the ones who make it move. Due to the magical force always moving through their forest, often times you can find things growing there you can't find growing anywhere else in the world."

"How strong are these guys?" Pelmor asked.

"I don't know, I never met them before. Besides, as long as we don't get caught it won't matter," Miko said.

"So, basically, we're going to go in there without a plan, hoping things go our way," Pelmor sighed.

"Why not? It worked out for us with the wizards," Miko shrugged.

"When we all die, don't anyone go blaming it on me," Pelmor dropped his shoulders, shaking his head.

"Don't worry so much, Pelmor, we'll be fine," Kelovin said. "I want to get a closer look at the forest, so let's go."

"Before we head there, I would like to explain another aspect of the Defra to you," Miko said. "I'm sure you noticed by now that the shade of the color of my hair fluctuates every now and then. This is because the particular shade a color is on a Defra

Elf's hair, the stronger that Elf is. The fluctuation is a representation of the emotion attached to your power changing your current power level. While we are in there, if you see a Defra with extremely dark green hair, then you would probably best run from that Elf rather than try to fight him. Of course, if everything goes to plan, we won't see and Defra anyway."

"Why would anyone broadcast their power like that?" Pelmor asked.

"Its not by choice. We're not sure why it works like that; all we know is that is how it works," Miko replied.

Kelovin let what Miko said sink in for a moment. There was so much about his people he still did not know. He would need to pursue more answers in the future. "Let's get going," Kelovin said.

The three of them took off running across the field. It did not take them long to get to the forest's edge. As they neared the forest, they slowed to a walk. The edge of the forest was clearly discernible from the rest of the land. The forest was at least a foot of dirt higher in both directions. Kelovin stepped up into the forest. He felt a small tugging sensation going backward. "You can actually feel it move," Kelovin called out.

"Why wouldn't you be able to? It's not called the Traveling Forest for no reason. Keep quiet, this is supposed to be a stealth mission," Miko said. Pelmor took a slow step up onto the forest, his eyebrows shooting up as he put his foot down. Miko looked to Pelmor and asked, "Can you do some cloaking spells around us, even if we are moving?"

"It will be harder to keep up, but I should be able to do it," Pelmor said, going straight into creating the necessary barriers. Once he was finished, he gave a nod to Miko.

"All right, let's try to do this quickly. Keep your eyes peeled. Once we find what we're looking for, we get out of here.

Trust me when I say we don't want to have to fight," Miko said. The three of them traveled inside the forest at a brisk pace.

Kelovin was admiring the bright colors all around them when Miko stopped abruptly in front of them saying, "Hold on..." He never got to finish his sentence as the vegetation around them sprang to life. Hundreds of vines rose up, shooting toward them. Miko sent out a wave of air around them. It ripped through the vines, making them all fall to the ground. Seconds later there was another wave coming at them.

"We need to run," Miko yelled. The path behind them was the densest with vines, so Miko shot deeper into the forest, sending torrents of wind in front of him to clear the path. Kelovin and Pelmor wasted no time in following him. Pelmor created a force shield behind them. Vines crashed into the invisible shield repeatedly as they tried to break through it.

Kelovin watched as a thick branch shot out sideways trapping Miko within its grip. He drew his sword without slowing, summoning strength to his arms as fast as he could. He chopped straight through the branch with ease. Miko recovered quickly, and he was out in the lead once more a moment later. Kelovin saw branches ahead of them begin weaving together to create a wall.

"Miko," Kelovin called ahead of him.

"I see it," Miko called back. "Run faster." They pushed on faster. The branches were expanding at a far greater rate than they were running. Miko sent a few waves of air at the wall. It proved to be too hard for the air to cut through. "Kelovin, get us through it," Miko yelled.

Kelovin raised his sword summoning all of the strength he could into his swing. His sword ripped through several of the branches before breaking at the hilt. Kelovin dropped the broken sword. He pounded against the wall with his magically enhanced fists. It cracked, groaning with each hit.

"Kelovin," he heard Pelmor cry out. He turned around to see his friends being engulfed by the grass at their feet. The grass beneath his own feet sprang to life, growing upwards at an incredible rate. He twisted trying to kick his feet out of it while simultaneously ripping at it with his hands. His efforts were getting him nowhere. No matter how much damage he did to it there was more to replace it. Flowers with thorns grew into the swirling mass, prodding him all over his body. He felt his body get heavy. His mind lost all focus. He realized the flowers must have been poison of some kind as the world went black.

Chapter Seven

"I knew I should never have listened to you!" Kelovin awoke to the sounds of shouting. He was still too disoriented to tell who or where it was coming from. "You've been trouble from the start. Now, thanks to you, we're all going to die. It was my responsibility to protect Kelovin. I was supposed to bring him home safely. I let you jeopardize all of it." He finally recognized the voice as Pelmor's. There was no response to Pelmor's accusations.

Kelovin let his eyes focus on his surroundings. They were in a small circle surrounded by extremely thick, interwoven trees. Their branches connected together to form a barrier to prevent escape. Pelmor was pacing back and forth while Miko sat against one of the trees. "I know things seem bad, but we'll get out of it," Miko said.

"What in this whole situation makes you think we'll escape? Look around, we're in the middle of a moving forest surrounded by people who obviously outclass us." Pelmor had stopped pacing to face Miko as he yelled.

"They do not outclass us, they simply outnumber us. They must have seen us approaching to be as prepared as they were for us to come. When we make our escape, they will not be so prepared," Miko said.

“How can you possibly know the only reason we were bested is because we were outnumbered? We never saw anyone. For all we know it could have been one person,” Pelmor continued to yell.

“Didn’t you notice how their attempts to capture us slowly became a little bit stronger the further we went? It’s because they slowly added people to the attempt to capture us. They would have started with the stronger stuff if they had been able to. Besides, I count this as us being lucky,” Miko said.

“How does any of this make us lucky?” Pelmor demanded to know.

“Because this, here, is the herb we came here looking for,” Miko said, picking the herb from the ground. “They put our jail right on top of what we came here for.”

Kelovin sat up, “Why would they put us on top of something so valuable?”

Pelmor turned toward Kelovin, "Kelovin, you're awake. Are you okay?”

“I'm fine. Right now, I'm only wondering why in the world something the wizards find so valuable would be in these Defra’s prison area,” Kelovin said.

“Perhaps to them, it’s more like a weed, a grows-everywhere type of thing, or they don't realize it has any value to someone else,” Miko said, shrugging his shoulders.

“I still don't see how we’re ever going to be able to get out of this place alive,” Pelmor said.

"I'm working on it. Be quiet, someone is coming," Miko said. The trees around them withdrew their branches to create an opening for two Defra Elves to walk through. They had green hair matching the color of the grass in the Great Plains. Their eyes were dark green.

"Get up," one of them commanded.

"Maybe if you ask me nicely," Miko said. "I'm feeling pretty comfortable down here."

The other Elf punched Miko across the face, "You will listen when you're spoken to."

"All right, all right, no need to get barbaric," Miko said. He smiled as he stood up. He made an exaggerated bow, "Where to, my lord?"

"You won't find yourself so funny when you're dying," the first Elf said. The captors led them out of the prison area to a large opening in the forest. There were dozens of Elves, all with different shades of green hair.

They were all dressed in various forms of plant life. Leaves appeared to be the most common. Many had bracelets of golden leaves running up their arms. Each individual Defra's bracelet had different numbers of leaves on them. He noticed most of the women were wearing crowns of flowers upon their heads as well. "Why aren't there any other kinds of Defra Elves?" Kelovin asked.

"This is a renegade group," Miko said, "They split off from the main village. Obviously, they only let certain people into their club." They were stopped in the middle of the clearing. The two Elves escorting them joined the others toward the outside edge of the clearing.

Another Elf stepped forward. His hair was a deep emerald color. "How kind of you to stop by, we haven't had visitors in so long we were beginning to get bored," the Elf said, "We've been itching to watch a good fight. Since all of you are Elves, we believe you should prove to be quite entertaining," He pointed toward Pelmor, "You shall be the first."

"No," Miko said, stepping forward. "I'm much more entertaining, anyway." Pelmor grabbed his shoulder to stop him. Miko shrugged him off, stepping farther forward.

The Elf threw his head back to laugh. When he stopped, he looked at Miko and said, "Eager to die, are we? Well, you're lucky I'm in a good mood. You can go first. Don't worry, there will be plenty of time to kill your companions after you've already died." Vines shot forward, grabbing Pelmor and Kelovin, securing them off to the side of the clearing.

"What should we do?" Pelmor whispered to Kelovin.

"There is nothing we can do. We're surrounded. They look prepared to deal with anything we try. We're going to have to watch to see what happens," Kelovin said.

"What if he dies?" Pelmor asked.

"If it looks like he is going to die, we'll do something, but not beforehand." Kelovin turned his attention back to Miko. He was standing in the middle of the clearing with a grin on his face.

From the other side of the forest, a tree holding a troll hostage walked into the middle of the clearing in front of Miko. There was a cheer from the crowd. The Elf who spoke before made a motion, causing the tree to go still. It released the troll from its grip. The troll roared, making the audience cheer again. The troll was ten feet tall. Its girth was huge; Kelovin thought the troll must weigh a ton.

The troll reached up to tear a large branch off of the tree previously holding him prisoner. With one last bellow of rage, the troll charged Miko. The ground shook with every step. Miko stood, waiting. Kelovin thought he might have even heard him laughing. Miko certainly was strange enough to do so. The troll swung his tree branch in a large sweeping arc over the ground.

Miko leaped over it, using the air to help propel him into a flip over the troll's head. As he passed above it, he gave the troll a pat on the head yelling, "Good troll." The crowd burst into laughter.

The troll roared again. It turned on Miko, once more charging recklessly toward him. Miko sent a large ball of rotating air at him. It connected high on the troll's right shoulder, sending him spiraling to his knees. The large tree branch dropped to the ground. Miko ran over to it. He used his air to support him so he could lift the tree branch up.

He was about to bring it crashing down on the troll's head when a fist made of grass sprung from the earth. It knocked Miko backward. Kelovin and Pelmor yelled that it was cheating. Their protests fell on deaf ears.

The lead Elf stepped forward, calling out so everyone could hear him, "We can't have you winning so easily. We came for a show, so a show is what we'll have. Release the other two." Two more trees walked out into the clearing, each holding trolls.

"Are you sure three is enough?" Miko called out. He bent down to pick up a rock. The first troll got back to his feet, charging Miko again. Miko danced out of its way. He threw his rock at one of the trolls being released from the tree. A gale force wind followed behind the rock to guide and speed it up. The troll wasn't ready for it. The rock bore into its eye. The troll squealed, clutching its eye as it stumbled backward with its other arm flailing about.

The first troll was on top of him again. It swung its huge fist at him. Miko jumped over it, simultaneously sending a ball of air beneath the troll's chin. The troll was lifted up off his feet. It grunted, thrashing its arm as though it were swimming in the air before falling onto its back.

Miko turned to see the third troll charging across the field after him. Miko ran to the large branch, lifting it up once more. He turned sideways to the troll, planting his feet firmly on the ground. Sweat trickled down his forehead while he waited for the troll to get close enough for him to swing.

The air around them screamed as large amounts of it was relocated all at once to power Miko's swing. The branch moved so fast, it turned into a blur. There was an ear-deafening crack. The branch exploded into pieces against the troll's head. The troll's body went limp. It fell to the ground with a tremendous thud. Its head was caved in like a crater where Miko hit.

The crowd of Defra Elves went wild cheering for Miko. Their leader stepped forward, "Enough!" The crowd fell silent. "Obviously, we have underestimated you, Elf. Next time, we'll prepare something more suited to your abilities. Take them away." A few of the green-haired Elves stepped forward to grab hold of all three of them. They were escorted back to their prison. The trees' branches grew back together once they were all within its confines.

"You were amazing," Kelovin said, staring at Miko. "How did you learn to fight the way you did back there?"

"Courtesy of the place I grew up in." Miko shrugged his shoulders before sitting against the tree in the same position he'd been in before. Miko looked at Pelmor, "You can communicate with the trees, can't you?"

"Yes," Pelmor answered.

"Can you talk to these ones?" Miko asked.

"I can try, sometimes it takes a while for them to respond, though," Pelmor said.

"I have a plan, but I need you to communicate with the trees. See what they think about their masters," Miko said.

"Okay," Pelmor said, moving to one of the trees. He placed his hand on top of it, took a deep breath, and closed his eyes.

Miko watched him for a few moments before turning to Kelovin, "You and I need to train your magic. We need your powers stronger if we're going to stand a chance of breaking out of here."

"You want me to practice with the rocks again?" Kelovin asked.

"No, there's no time for accuracy training now, you'll have to skip ahead. Your powers have a unique ability to nullify the magic of others. It will drain strength out of your own magic at the same time, so you have to get better at summoning large quantities of strength in short periods of time," Miko said.

"So, what do you want me to do?" Kelovin asked.

"I'm going to make a compact force of air above the ground with a branch underneath it. Your job will be to break through using your magic to weaken mine. You need to be able to break the branch beneath in one swing. When you're swinging, concentrate on absorbing the magic in front of you." Miko placed a branch on the ground. He looked at the spot for a moment before saying, "Okay, go ahead."

Kelovin's eyebrows squinted together. He felt his magical strength pooling into his arms. "Swing," Miko's voice commanded. Kelovin punched downwards. The air in front of his fist felt as if it were rubber as his punch was slowed to a stop then tossed backward. The air barrier was far more resistant than he realized.

"You did not concentrate on absorbing the magic," Miko said.

"I was still concentrating on gathering strength when you told me to swing," Kelovin protested.

"I told you, you must be able to do this quickly. In a fight, you don't have forever. Do it again," Miko said.

They repeated the process for several hours until Kelovin was too exhausted to keep going. When Miko told him to rest, he flopped onto the ground. He was depressed by the results he'd had while practicing. He never once even got close to getting through Miko's air barrier. To make it worse, Miko had informed him he had never managed to absorb even a small part of his magic. No matter how hard he concentrated on doing what Miko told him to do, he could not pull it off. He wasn't sure he would ever be able to do it. While he was on the ground, reflecting on his failure, he noticed it was starting to get dark. He looked over to see Pelmor in the same position as he'd been several hours ago.

Kelovin stayed on the ground, letting time pass him by. He needed some rest anyway. It was because he was on his back staring upward that he noticed the branches of the trees surrounding them growing food. The fruit grew until it reached full maturity, then dropped to the ground around them. "This must be the way they feed their prisoners," Miko said, grabbing a piece of fruit. He ate it without hesitation.

"Wait, what if they poisoned it?" Kelovin asked.

"If they wanted to kill us, they would have done so already," Miko said. "They want to see the battles. It's the only reason we're still alive." Kelovin couldn't see any fault in his logic, so he picked up a couple of pieces of fruit. He hadn't seen fruit like it before. They were juicy with a sweet flavor. Their outsides were green, their insides yellow.

"You'd better sleep and get your strength back, we're going to be doing more exercises once you're up," Miko said.

"Okay," Kelovin said. He looked over to where Pelmor sat with his hand against the tree. He hadn't moved at all. Kelovin decided not to bother him. He lay back on the ground to go to sleep. His body was exhausted, so it wasn't hard to do.

He awoke to Miko prodding him. "Let's go. Get up, no time to waste," Miko said. The sky was still dark. Kelovin groaned. His body still felt exhausted. Miko spoke again, "Nope, there is no complaining from people who are imprisoned." Kelovin sat up, rubbing the sleep from his eyes. He looked over to see Pelmor still sitting in his same position. Seeing his dedication gave Kelovin energy.

"What are we doing? Same thing as yesterday?" Kelovin asked, rising to his feet.

"Same concept, different method," Miko said. "You're going to try to land a punch on me while I use air to deflect your hits. You want to concentrate on absorbing the magic so your punches will keep going forward rather than being tossed to the side."

"Are you sure? I don't want to hurt you," Kelovin said.

Miko laughed, "Don't worry. You're not even going to touch me if you keep going the way you were yesterday." Kelovin concentrated his strength to his arms and swung. Wind slammed against his arm, sending him sprawling to the side. "You need to keep a stronger stance when attacking someone," Miko said.

They continued with the exercise until mid-day. They took small breaks every so often to let Kelovin catch his breath. They were on one such break, about to continue again, when the branches receded. Kelovin shot a look at Pelmor, still sitting at the tree. Kelovin did not want them to see what Pelmor was doing. Pelmor was too far out of his reach for Kelovin to tap his shoulder as a warning. He could see the Defra approaching them already, so he didn't dare move at the risk of drawing unwanted attention toward Pelmor.

His worry was abated when Pelmor broke his position right before the Defra were within sight of him. It was the same two as before. One spoke, "Let's go. It's time to fight again."

As they were being led back to the clearing, Pelmor leaned over to whisper to Miko and Kelovin, "The tree finally spoke to me when those guys came to get us."

"Good, we'll talk about it after I kill whatever they think is going to pose a challenge," Miko said.

"No talking." One of the Elves gave Miko a shove. They arrived back into the clearing. Kelovin thought there might be more Elves there this time. It was too hard to tell for sure. Miko was led to the middle, while vines restrained Kelovin and Pelmor off to the side again.

The apparent leader stepped forward to speak, "I trust you're well rested? We don't want this fight to end too quickly now."

"If it's anything like the last fight, I don't think you have to worry about me being the reason this fight ends early," Miko smirked.

"Oh, no, this fight is going to be much more interesting. You see we came upon another intruder today. I think he may be able to give us a good show." Another Defra Elf was dragged into the clearing. This one had brown hair the color of dirt. His eyes were a dark brown.

"Well, this should certainly be interesting," Miko said.

"Bright Eyes, I can't believe after all this time, I finally have the pleasure of killing you," the Brown Defra Elf said.

"Trug, I can't believe after all this time, you still think you can actually best me," Miko called back.

"I'm not the same weak boy you remember. We're not kids anymore, Bright Eyes." Trug slammed his fist into the ground. Miko jumped sideways, barely dodging a spike of earth erupting from the ground.

"No, I guess we're not, but your rocks are as slow as ev..." Miko was stopped mid-sentence by a rock slamming into his back. The force sent him tumbling forward. He slowly picked himself back up.

"I've learned a few things over the years, Bright Eyes. Like I said, you won't find me as weak as I once was." Miko sent out a wave of air around him. Through it, he could feel several more rocks floating around him waiting to strike.

Miko grinned, "Looks like this is going to be a much more interesting fight than I thought. Unfortunately, you're still mad if you think you're going to best me." Trug roared in frustration. He sent three of his floating rocks at Miko from three different directions. It was exactly what Miko wanted him to do.

He jumped to the side into a roll. While on the ground, Miko grabbed a solid-looking stick. He came out of the roll to his feet, throwing the stick. He used his air to speed up and focus its flight. Trug tried to evade by twisting out of its way but too slowly. It pierced into Trug's shoulder. Trug cried out in surprise, clutching his shoulder.

Trug chuckled to himself. He straightened up and said, "So, you've learned how to throw a real punch, Bright Eyes."

“Apparently I underestimated you a little bit,” Miko taunted. “I thought I was already going to kill you.”

Trug sent three more rocks at Miko. Miko grinned; Trug never did seem to be a fast learner. Miko rolled to the side to dodge again. This time in mid-roll, a large rock shot out of the ground at him. Miko drew air in to create a cushion. His reflexes proved too slow. The rock smashed into his chest. It sent him sprawling backward.

Miko groaned on the ground. He’d been using too much energy training Kelovin. He knew he couldn't let this fight continue much longer, or his energy would be spent completely. Miko grinned, "You still are no match for me, Trug, even with all the great progress you’ve made in my absence."

"You and I must be fighting two different fights, Bright Eyes," Trug bellowed. He stomped his foot, sending a dozen more rocks up around him. Miko closed his eyes. He needed to concentrate to gather in enough wind for his next attack. Kelovin noticed the air around them getting thicker. Miko continued to draw air in until he felt Trug begin to make his move.

Miko immediately sent the air into a swirling vortex with Trug at its center. Trug let out a yell of surprise as a powerful cyclone appeared around him. The force of it caught the rocks in mid-flight, sending them scattering in different directions. Miko continued to feed the cyclone power until it lifted Trug off the ground. The debris picked up by the winds cut at Trug, tearing into his skin. From within the cyclone, he roared in frustration. As the winds became more violent, Trug started to plead for mercy.

With a final grunt of effort from Miko, the twister threw Trug out headfirst into a tree. Trug's lifeless body fell to the ground with a dull thump. The Defra Elves surrounding them erupted into cheers at the show of power– all except the leader, who glared at Miko. Miko sat on the ground, clearly exhausted. Miko still managed to smile up at the leader.

"Take them back to the prison," the leader demanded. The guards immediately jumped up to take them back to their cell. When they were out of sight of the cheering crowd, one of the guards spoke. "You're stronger than we thought. Your death will be much more interesting than I anticipated."

"Ha, you still think you can find something you can kill me with. I'll destroy everything you throw at me," Miko said.

"It is only a matter of time before you will tire and not be able to fight anymore. In any case, you will be here until you die, so it does not matter how many you win. The result will still be the same." The guards threw them into the circle of trees and left.

Miko's legs gave out. His body slumped to the ground. Kelovin ran over to him. He said, "We can't let you keep fighting, you're too exhausted."

"No," Miko grinned, "I'm the best chance in the ring for all of us to survive. Besides, we need you to work on your strength and Pelmor to work on the trees, so I need to fight."

"Then, at least don't taunt them so much. You make them want to try even harder to find someone capable of killing you," Kelovin said.

"No. We need them to think I'm so confident in my ability to win that I'm not thinking about running away. Let's talk about more important things, like what Pelmor was able to get from the tree when he spoke to it," Miko said.

Pelmor looked up to say, "Not too much. Basically, it acknowledged my presence and showed me its anger with the other Elves. They don’t like the abusive control the Elves exercise over them."

"So, you will be able to convince it to help us escape?" Miko asked.

"Eventually, probably. It will be a slow process," Pelmor said, then added in explanation, "Trees are already normally slow in making decisions. These decisions will be made even harder by the magical control imposed by the Elves."

"Well, in the meantime, I guess we need to keep up your practice, Kelovin," Miko said, beginning to rise.

"No," Pelmor put a hand on his shoulder, "You need to rest for the next fight. I will not need to spend so much time connected to the tree, so I will help Kelovin train. You can give me instructions on how to train him."

"He's right, you need as much rest as you can get," Kelovin said.

Miko held up his hands, "All right, I surrender. You're probably right, anyway." Miko slumped back to the ground. "You have the magical shield, don't you, Pelmor?" Miko asked.

"Yeah," Pelmor said.

"For now, create one wherever you want while Kelovin tries to break through using both his damper magic and his strength." Pelmor nodded, so Miko turned his attention to Kelovin. "I wish I could explain how to access your power better, but, as I said, I was never trained as a Strength Defra, so you'll have to figure it out. All I can say is try to focus." When Kelovin nodded, Miko closed his eyes.

“Miko,” Kelovin said. Miko reopened his eyes, so Kelovin continued, “Why was Trug calling you Bright Eyes? You knew him before, right? There’s no other way you could have known his name.”

“I don’t like talking much about my past, it disturbs me,” Miko said. Kelovin waited for him to say something more. After a short pause, Miko did. “I’ll give you a brief explanation. I grew up in the Black Defra’s village. If you live there, it is be evil or be tortured until you’re evil. The eyes of a Defra Elf are unique compared to other races. They literally reflect your inner desires. If you are good-natured on the inside, your eyes turn to a lighter shade. If you’re evil-natured, they turn darker. Mine turned lighter, thus the nickname Bright Eyes and the reason everyone hated me so I left.” Miko closed his eyes to indicate he was finished talking about it.

Kelovin stared for a moment to let it all sink in. He had more questions he wanted to be answered. It was clear, however, that now was not a good time to talk about it. He turned to Pelmor and said, “Let’s get started then.”

Pelmor created a force shield over the ground. He pointed to it and said, "All right, go for it." Kelovin nodded. He walked over to where Pelmor pointed. He gave an experimental nudge at the spot Pelmor indicated. An unseen force about half a foot above the ground stopped his finger. Kelovin knelt into position by the spot. He concentrated the best he could. He tried to tell his magic to absorb the magic in front of him. He swung as hard as he could. The force shield stopped him cold. He frowned at his results. He continued trying for hours until both he and Pelmor were exhausted.

Chapter Eight

Kelovin couldn't recall how many days had passed since they were captured. After a week, the days had started blending together for him. All he did every day was train, eat, and watch Miko dispatch whatever the Defra could throw at him. They made him fight every day against whatever they could find. He was lucky there were many days when they couldn't produce anything challenging for him. Those days, Miko would help with Kelovin's training. He always made sure not to overextend himself in training, so he would be prepared the next day if he faced something or someone stronger than normal. The continuous fighting took a toll on Miko's energy.

Kelovin understood how exhausted he must be. The constant exercises he did sapped his own strength. Miko helped with the training while fighting various things. He could only imagine how hard it must be. The strange thing was, even with the feeling he couldn't go forward another inch, he felt stronger than he ever had before.

"Try again," Miko said in his usual slumped position against one of the trees. Kelovin stared at the spot before him. He did not know how many times he'd tried to break through the barrier between him and the ground–probably millions. No matter what he did, he could not make his magic absorb the strength of either Miko's or Pelmor's magic. He stayed still, thinking about his own magic. Whenever he used it, it felt like a constant flow of strength he channeled through his body. The flow kept whatever magical attack he was using going. He assumed it was the same for Pelmor and Miko.

The problem was, they both had been training with magic far longer than he had. Their flow was too powerful for him to hope to overcome. Even if he was supposed to naturally have a larger flow as a Strength Defra, he was too far behind for it to matter. Kelovin smiled. Perhaps he had been concentrating on the wrong thing.

He swung as hard as he could. He felt the resistance of Pelmor's force shield, but only for a moment. His fist smashed straight through the shield. It left his arm sunken a couple of inches into the ground. Miko jumped up, pumping his fist into the air, "All right, Kelovin, that's what I'm talking about."

Pelmor stared blankly in surprise, "Your attack felt strange. It was like I was cut off from my shield." Kelovin grinned in triumph. "How did you do it?" Pelmor asked.

"I had a hunch I'd been focusing on doing the wrong thing this entire time. I've been trying to absorb your magic this whole time. It's like trying to suck away your entire flow of magic. It wasn't going to happen. I decided it would be easier to focus on cutting off your flow to the force shield instead."

"Seriously?" Miko asked, "I'm pretty sure I've never heard of someone else cutting off magic flow before. I think they normally overwhelm the system because of their incredible strength while at the same time weakening the other's magic with the absorption. Here, try to do it against my air so I can see what it feels like. Then I'll know if it's different."

"All right, let's give it a go," Kelovin said. Kelovin readied himself. As soon as Miko nodded to him, he swung again. Once again, he felt the initial resistance, then it was gone, and his hand smashed into the ground.

"Wow," Miko said. "This is incredible. I did not even know it was possible."

"You're telling me after having these powers for centuries, none of the others figured out how to use it this way?" Kelovin asked.

"Well, I guess I am. It's always taught the same way, no one questions it. I guess my statement to you before is even truer than I thought. Your magic is only limited by your imagination. I think we're ready for our escape now. We should be able to do it today, right after the fight. They will be the least prepared to intercept us if we do it then," Miko said.

"Good, because I'm tired of being in this forest," Pelmor grumbled.

"Are you sure the trees will help us escape?" Miko asked.

"They will do their best," Pelmor said. "They say it's not easy to mask our movement from their masters. They have assured me they will try to at least give us a head start." From Pelmor's conversations with the trees, they had found out the Defra were sensitive to any movement within the forest. They usually had someone monitoring the area of the prison closely for any attempts at escape.

They did not have to wait long for the guards to come get them for the day's fight. "Let's go, you know the drill," one of them said.

"What do I get to kill today?" Miko asked, hopping to his feet eagerly.

The two guards laughed, "Oh I don't think you will be so happy today. This could be the day you die." They continued laughing.

"Nothing you've sent me has even come close so far. You think you can actually give me something capable of killing me?" Miko put his hand to his chest in mock fear, "Oh my, do save me from this evil."

"We'll see who is laughing soon enough, air scum," the guard sneered. They were led back to the usual clearing with all of their captors waiting anxiously for a fight. The leader stood apart from the rest with a satisfied smile on his face. The three of them were left standing in the middle. "Why didn't they take us to the side as usual?" Pelmor asked in a whisper.

"I don't know. I don't like this. Something different is about to happen," Miko said.

The leader stepped forward, "We have decided three prisoners are too many mouths to feed, so the three of you will fight until only one remains."

"I see you're tired of trying to find things for me to kill. Well, I'm not fighting them," Miko said, sitting down. Kelovin and Pelmor followed his example.

"If you do not fight, then we will kill all of you," The leader said.

"Go ahead, see if I care," Miko smiled.

The leader raised his hand to motion the guards to kill them. Someone from the crowd yelled, "Find something else for them to fight. We want to see a real fight." The rest of the crowd took up similar calls. Soon, the whole place was yelling their displeasure.

The leader raised his hands for silence, "I thought you might feel this way. I prepared a special fight for this as well." He motioned to some unseen Defra. Moments later, from the edges of the clearing all around them, twenty large beasts were brought out. They were long black cats, each with powerful legs and large mouths. The leader continued once all of the cats were in sight, "If you don't fight each other, then you will have to face all of these at once."

Miko laughed, "You sorely underestimate our abilities if you think we're scared of a bunch of cats."

Pelmor whispered, "They look pretty intimidating to me."

Miko whispered back, "Don't worry, on the open field these things are not as impressive as they look."

"So be it," the leader grinned, "Comrades, I think it is time for a field change." The entire crowd went quiet. The edges of the clearing shook violently.

Everyone on the outskirts of the clearing rose fifteen feet into the air on top of a wall of vegetation. "Wow," Kelovin gasped. Their surroundings went silent again for a moment. Then, Kelovin and his group had to move out of the way as trees and bushes sprouted out of the ground around them.

"This could be worse than I thought," Miko said. "Don't worry. All we need to do is stick together." Kelovin and Pelmor nodded grimly. Most of the growth only came up to their necks to allow the spectators full access to see things happening while still giving ample cover for the cats to hide in.

The leader walked forward, a bridge of vines growing beneath his feet. When he stood partway out into the clearing fifteen feet above their heads, he spoke, "We shall see if you are as truly talented as you believe today. Release the cats." He waved a signal as he said it. He strolled back to the perimeter in triumph.

"Okay, new plan," Miko said. "We're leaving right now. After all the magic they used to do this, they will be weaker than usual. We can use our surroundings as cover. We'll have to reach the west side of the clearing first."

"Don't we want to go south?" Kelovin asked.

"No. Remember, the forest has been moving this whole time. By now, we are pretty far east of the wizards' tower," Miko said.

"I assume there is no real plan here," Pelmor sighed.

"Come on, you know by now our best plans are no plans," Miko smiled. "Follow my lead. Keep a lookout for hungry cats."

"I can throw up a shield around us," Pelmor offered.

"No. Holding up one big enough will take too much energy. We're in this for the long haul. We need to conserve as much energy as we can. Only throw one up if you have to."

"It has become too quiet," Kelovin said. He looked up and noticed the spectators surrounding them were watching intently. "I think there is one of them nearby."

Miko sent out a wave of air, "You're right. There are three of them surrounding us, actually. Get ready." Kelovin summoned his strength magic, letting it flow through his whole body until he knew where it was needed. When one of the cats leaped out of a bush at him, he sent the magic down his arm and swung. He caught the cat on the side of the face, sending it sprawling sideways.

He turned to see Miko and Pelmor engaged with the other two cats. Miko's cat was leaping side-to-side in order to dodge the various things he was hurling at it. Pelmor's cat was stalking around him, presumably trying to figure out what was stopping him from getting to the Elf. A vine snaked out, catching the cat by the leg. The large cat was yanked off its feet.

Kelovin took the opportunity to run over. As he reached it, the cat was thrashing about as the grass tried to imprison him. Kelovin sent his magic through his whole arm, smashing it down onto the cat's head. There was a loud crunch as the skull caved in.

"Kelovin, watch out," Pelmor said. Kelovin was about to turn when the cat he'd hit earlier jumped on top of him, bringing him to the ground. Kelovin threw his elbow backward. All he felt was air. His poorly aimed swing was rewarded with claws raking down his back. He panicked, causing a surge of strength magic to converge in his back. He felt a gush of air rush past him. The weight on top of him disappeared. Kelovin scrambled to his feet in time to see Pelmor send a levitated rock into the cat's head. Miko stood close by. The third cat's body was behind him, full of branches.

"Are you okay?" Pelmor asked, running over.

"Yeah, I'm fine. I can hardly feel it," Kelovin said.

"Let me close it up, at least," Pelmor said, walking up to him. Kelovin turned his back toward him. "This is strange," Pelmor said.

"What is?" Kelovin asked.

"The wound on your back stops partway down, as though the cat's claws hit something hard," Pelmor said.

"Are you serious?" Kelovin asked.

"You mean you never thought about using your magic defensively? Defense is one of the greatest strengths your type of magic has. You have the capability of making your body harder than rocks or absorbing oncoming magical attacks. After you've mastered absorbing them, anyway," Miko said.

Pelmor laid his hands on top of Kelovin's back. Kelovin could feel the wound stop bleeding. "I've stopped the bleeding, but I'm afraid I can't do much more than that right now without expending too much energy," Pelmor said.

"That will do just fine," Kelovin said.

Pelmor turned his attention to Miko and asked, "Why can't he stop magical attacks now? I thought he already achieved the ability to do so during training today?"

"Cutting off a magical attack's flow of energy won't necessarily stop the attack every time. Some attacks are powerful enough to keep going," Miko said. He glanced around, "They were only testing our strength with those three. We need to get moving because next time they attack it will be with all of them."

"All right, lead the way," Kelovin said. Miko took off at a trot to the west. They were not far from the clearing edge. The clearing itself was only several hundred feet wide.

When they approached the wall, Miko called out softly, "There are two more friends ahead of us. Kelovin and I will take them out as quickly as we can. Pelmor, you go politely ask the tree to move without alerting our captors. Once it's done, we need to be invisible."

"I'm on it," Pelmor said. Miko pointed a direction and Pelmor ran toward the plant wall.

"All right, our friends are just ahead over there," Miko said pointing the opposite direction.

"Let's go give them a fight, then," Kelovin grinned.

"I like your spirit," Miko said, laughing louder than normal. He glanced upward at the spectators before continuing in a lower voice, "Remember we need to kill them quickly; the other cats are close on our backs."

Kelovin charged forward toward the bushes the cats were apparently hiding in, though he couldn't see them. As he got closer, a cat leaped out of the bushes. Kelovin stepped sideways, kicking it in the ribs, assisted by his magical strength, as it passed by. There were loud cracks as the cat's chest collapsed inward. Kelovin gave it one more kick to make sure it was dead. Its neck snapped backward with a sickening crunch.

Kelovin turned to see that the other cat was gone. Miko stood grinning from ear to ear. He pointed up. Above, there was a scene of commotion and confusion.

"I decided they wanted to play too, so I gave the cat a lift to the top," Miko said. When Kelovin looked back down, he couldn't see Miko anymore.

Kelovin jumped when he heard Pelmor's voice next to him, "Good distraction Miko, we're ready to go."

Kelovin nodded before he realized that his friends probably couldn't see it anyway. He ran toward where Pelmor had gone before. He found a small hole in the wall leading the way out. He squeezed through it. On the other side, Miko and Pelmor were waiting, once again visible.

"After the crowd figures out we're gone, we'll only have about a minute's head start before the trees won't be able to mask our movement," Pelmor said.

"Hopefully, we won't need any longer," Miko said.

"There is good news. Somehow, we're fortunate enough to have their weapons stash not far ahead of us," Pelmor said.

"All right, let's get out of here. Pelmor, lead the way," Kelovin said. Pelmor took off at a run. Kelovin took one last glance behind him before following. He saw the hole in the wall had closed up behind them.

It only took a few seconds to get to a huge tree with hundreds of weapons sticking out of its bark. During the weeks of training, the forest had revealed to Pelmor the location of various things within its borders. Kelovin scanned the blades until he found a one-handed sword made of good steel. The scabbard hung from the sword. He grabbed it and took a couple of practice swings to make sure it was what he wanted. He turned to Pelmor. Pelmor had chosen a similar sword.

"Okay, we need to go straight west. If we have to, we can go south a bit too," Miko said.

Pelmor led them sprinting as fast he could through the forest. Kelovin and Miko followed right behind him. Kelovin was getting hopeful for success when they'd been running for a couple of minutes without any struggle. He didn't let the hope take away from his focus on their surroundings. He still knew their chances of getting out without a fight was slim. Pelmor confirmed his fears when he called out, "The trees are giving their warning signal. The Defra are on our tails. Keep a watch for attacks."

Almost as if Pelmor had summoned them, vines snaked out from around them. The vines tried to trip their legs to stop their progress. Their pace slowed as they focused on dodging the attacks. Kelovin slid to a stop as they came face-to-face with a towering wall of vines. Pelmor ran up to it to hack parts of it down. He soon saw it was futile. The vines grew back faster than he could hack them down. Some of them snapped out at him, forcing him to retreat.

Miko sent a wave of air at it. As soon as he did, a few vines from different spots shot out to meet the wave, breaking up the wind slice before it could hit the wall. Kelovin summoned as much magic as he could. He swung his blade, using the strength to attack the vines' flow of magic. A portion of the wall fell to the ground, allowing them to continue past it. Their victory was short-lived. Another wall sprung up in front of them. This time, when Kelovin tried to approach, he was attacked by other vines from opposite directions. They were forced to go on the defensive.

"Kelovin, watch out," Pelmor called. Kelovin turned in time to see a spear-like vine aimed at his back being deflected by a force shield.

"Tha..." Kelovin began to say, but as he glanced backward, he saw another vine catch Pelmor while he was distracted. It went through his back and out of his chest. Pelmor fell to the ground. Kelovin ran to his side. Miko closed in next to them to continue battling off the vines.

"Pelmor, you need to heal yourself. I can't do it," Kelovin said.

"I can't," Pelmor gasped. "It's...too...painful."

"No, I won't allow you to die too. You have to live. Push past it," Kelovin pleaded, his voice quivering.

"Kelovin...Listen," Pelmor began between gasps, "I was...wrong. You must...continue... find yourself. Don't go...home...not yet. Find...the crystal."

"You can help me find it. All you have to do is reach out to gather magic. Heal yourself," Kelovin screamed. Pelmor was no longer there to hear him. His eyes were already glazed over. His breathing had stopped.

"Kelovin, I need your help," Miko called, as he battled vines shooting out from all directions.

"I want you all to burn," Kelovin whispered, almost to himself. He felt intense rage coursing through him, causing his body to shake. Specks of red flamed to life in his eyes and hair, making a tie-dye of red and gold. He felt a new feeling of magic enter his system. It felt hot and wild. He channeled it by instinct. He yelled louder, "I will burn you all."

Flames leaped from his hands, consuming the surrounding vines. The fire continued to grow, devouring everything around it. Miko sent air rushing in to make the flames spread faster. Soon, there was a blazing inferno.

"You need to make us an opening," Miko yelled. Kelovin ran forward straight toward the flames. The flames moved out of his way. Miko was behind him, barely getting through the flames before they closed back up. Kelovin saw one of the Green Defra outside the flames standing in his path. There was a look of horror on the Elf’s face. The red in Kelovin’s hair took on a darker color. Kelovin roared and threw a punch with all the strength he could summon. The Elf's skull shattered on impact. The force of

Kelovin's punch lifted the Elf's body from the ground and threw it several feet. Kelovin looked for another person, but Miko was there pulling him forward.

"We have to go, Kelovin. There are too many of them. They're panicked now; we must get the rest of the way out of here," Miko yelled in his face. Kelovin let his body be guided by Miko's pulling. They ran westward once more. He couldn't accept that Pelmor was gone. Pelmor had been his loyal friend from the beginning. He was the one who always supported him, even when he didn't want to. Kelovin's mind screamed at him to turn around in order to kill the rest of the Elves and rescue Pelmor. His feet kept following Miko out of the forest.

They made it out of the forest a couple of minutes later. They had been so close to escaping cleanly. They continued for another mile before Miko slowed to a stop. "We'll be fine here. They won't dare attack us on open ground. They would suffer too many casualties," he said.

Kelovin dropped to his knees. Tears rolled down his cheeks. "This is all my fault," Kelovin whispered.

"No, this is their fault. They're the ones who killed Pelmor," Miko said.

"No. I'm the one who dragged him out here. I'm the one he died trying to protect," Kelovin yelled.

"I'm sorry you lost Pelmor," Miko said. "I was starting to like the guy, myself. Sometimes we lose the people we love. There isn't anything we can do to change it. All we can do is try to keep them in our hearts as we keep living because it's what they would want us to do."

Kelovin didn't respond or move, so Miko sat down. After a moment Miko's stomach growled. He sent out airwaves in search of food. There wasn't much close, only a single rabbit. He decided it would have to do. Miko picked his way toward the rabbit, pulled a knife he'd taken from the tree, and threw it, aided by the wind, into the rabbit's head. He took the rabbit back to where Kelovin sat to cook the rabbit. Miko stopped partway through. He looked at Kelovin and asked, "I wanted to hold off asking you since your friend died, but who are you really?"

Kelovin looked up, startled by the question. "What do you mean?"

"You claim to never have known your powers before. It doesn't seem possible anymore. Back there, you pulled out fire magic like you'd been using it all your life. I'm pretty sure there's something you're not telling me," Miko said.

Kelovin shook his head, "No, I don't know where it came from. I'm not even sure how I did it. I couldn't do it right now, even if I tried."

"I suppose I believe you. After all, you broke your hand trying to punch a tree," Miko said thoughtfully. Silence fell between them again. Miko continued to prepare the rabbit. He used the wind to seek out stray pieces of firewood. Usually, the Traveling Forest left plenty behind. Time passed in silence as Miko finished all the preparations for their food. When he held out a portion to Kelovin, Miko was surprised to see him take it.

Kelovin set the rabbit down in front of him. He locked eyes with Miko. "You asked who I am. Before, I was a naïve child who thought the world was full of great adventure. I'm not going to be the same child anymore. I'm going to become the next king of my people. Before I do, I am going to bring back one of the crystal artifacts my father seeks. After I'm king, in the future, I'm going to put an end to people like the ones who killed Pelmor–starting with them. I'm going to make this world a better place. Will you help me?"

"I will as long as you're still on the right side in the end," Miko smiled. "I'm not going to follow a maniac. It wouldn't be good for my reputation, you know."

Kelovin couldn't bring himself to give Miko even a pretend grin, so instead, he said, "Thank you. Pelmor was my best friend. He did what my master did before him, he died protecting me. I must become strong enough to be able to protect those I love, instead of needing them to protect me. I am going to need to keep training." Kelovin reached up to feel the amulet he'd made from Ryga's message.

"Simple enough. I will do everything I can," Miko said.

Kelovin nodded. He picked up his portion of rabbit and ate. After a few bites, he paused to speak, "After we're finished here, we need to go get our information from the wizards."

"Agreed," Miko said. "I'm looking forward to seeing Raizen squirm when he's forced to divulge his information."

Kelovin went back to eating. He was trying desperately to keep his feelings in check. If he could focus on moving forward, perhaps he could make it through this. He focused his mind on eating the food.

When he was finished, he said, "How far away do you think it is to their tower?"

"I would guess not more than three or four hours," Miko said.

Kelovin rose from his seat, "Shall we get going? If we get started now, we should be able to make it there before dark."

"All right," Miko said, leaping to his feet. Kelovin set out at a brisk run west. A few hours later, the valley with the impossibly large tower came into view. Kelovin and Miko ran straight up to the doors. The doors swung open for them of their own accord as they approached.

"Looks like they saw us coming," Miko said.

They walked into the tower. Inside, the wizard who greeted them the first time was waiting. "Mystic Lord Raizen is waiting for you," the wizard said, opening the multicolored door. Miko looked at Kelovin, but he was already striding for the door. Miko shook his head. It was obvious Pelmor's death had shaken Kelovin. He needed to learn how to deal with it. It wasn't as if Pelmor dying didn't bother Miko, but he didn't show it because he'd become used to death early on in his life. He had become numb to it over the years. Miko followed Kelovin through the door. He hoped the oath they'd made Raizen take did its job. Otherwise, their whole trip had been for nothing.

Raizen was smiling when they entered the chamber. His smile widened when Miko pulled out the herbs he'd asked for. "I must say, I'm impressed you made it back. I wasn't expecting your success, to be honest. I see you are down by one. Too bad. I do give my sympathies."

Kelovin tensed up, the red in his hair went darker. Miko laid his hand on Kelovin's shoulder and whispered, "Now is not a good time for a fight. If we start something, we may be killed. He's the only one who took the oath, the other wizards will have no qualms killing us after he is dead."

Kelovin spoke to Raizen through gritted teeth, "We held up our end of the bargain, now tell us what you know about the other artifacts."

Raizen's grin somehow became even bigger, "I do..." Raizen let out screams of pain. His body dropped to the ground convulsing.

"Is this because of the oath?" Miko whispered.

"Yes," Kelovin said loudly so Raizen could hear as well. "The pain does not go away until you intend to fulfill your end of the oath."

"Okay," Raizen gasped between screams of pain. The pain subsided, leaving Raizen shaking on the ground. After a few minutes, he slowly rose from the ground. His smile was completely gone. "This is much more potent magic than I anticipated. I thought I had managed to protect myself from its effects. I may have to learn how to use it myself." Anger burned in his eyes as he paused for a moment. "It seems you have won this round. You had better be careful in the future. We do not take kindly to being outsmarted. We do not know much about the other artifacts. All we have are many rumors. The most promising location is south, to the uncharted lands. There is a village directly south from the human city. It is said they know the whereabouts of one of them. We ourselves have been meaning to go check it out. Unfortunately, the uncharted lands are dangerous. We don't have the resources to go ourselves at this moment. I don't have any other information about the artifacts."

"Thank you," Kelovin said turning to leave. "I look forward to seeing you again."

"Don't you want to make sure he doesn't know anything else?" Miko asked.

"No. If he knew more and withheld it, he would be in pain right now. The oath was to tell us everything," Kelovin said.

"Good enough for me," Miko said and followed Kelovin toward the exit.

Kelovin opened the magical door to the outside. He was about to leave when Raizen called out from behind them, "I hope your friend died as painfully as you will die one day."

Kelovin stopped midstep. His hands clenched. His red hair turned darker to the shade of a wildflower. He felt Miko's hand on his shoulder again. "Don't let what he says get to you, Kelovin. We can't fight right now."

Kelovin heard what Miko said, but it felt like his words were so far away. He channeled magical strength into his shoulder. He swung before he could think about what he was doing. He sent the strength through his arm as he swung exactly the way Miko had taught him. "Stop," Raizen's shrill voice called out.

His fist slammed into the wizard's magical door. The door reverberated, absorbing his attack. He couldn't break it. He already knew he wouldn't be able to. Dwarven magic is strong. Because Kelovin knew it wouldn't break, he'd focused most of the magic into snipping the doors magical bonds to all of the rooms in the tower.

He knew the relieved look on Raizen's face would only be temporary. He slammed the door closed. The multicolored door changed to the front gate before his eyes once it was closed. "Are you crazy? You'll have every wizard in the tower coming down on us, even without Raizen commanding them," Miko said.

"Only if they can remember the way out. I cut most of the door's pathways to their rooms," Kelovin said.

"Are you serious?" Miko asked. Kelovin nodded. Miko only stood staring at him in response. Kelovin turned south toward Eaglepoint. He only made it a few steps before the ground shook, causing him to stumble.

"What's going on?" Kelovin asked.

"One of the tower's defenses being activated. We need to go now before they get more turned on," Miko said. They ran for the south hill leading out of the valley. The ground continued to shake, trying to knock them off balance.

They started their climb up the hill at a frantic pace. Off to one side, an earth golem removed itself from the hill. "Run faster," Miko yelled. Kelovin felt the wind start pushing against his back. He dared a quick look behind him. The golem lifted a large boulder off the ground. It threw the boulder straight at them.

"Move," Kelovin said. He veered off to the right, making sure Miko did as well. The boulder narrowly missed them. They reached the top of the hill. The chaos around them calmed down. They ran until the tower was far behind them.

They slowed to a walk. Miko said, "We're lucky. Most of the wizards' defenses are designed to keep people from getting in not out."

"We should find somewhere we can rest for the night," Kelovin said.

"We should talk about making rash decisions after we've already won. I admit it's awesome you were able to create so much chaos for them. You still shouldn't have put us at so much unnecessary risk," Miko said.

"He pissed me off," Kelovin said. He narrowed his eyes, saying, "Aren't you the one who is always doing things without a plan, not thinking of the consequences."

"I've never done something unnecessary. I've only gone into similar situations because we needed something," Miko said. His voice softened, "I'm sorry we lost Pelmor. You have to know it wasn't my fault. You would've gone there anyway."

"Well, it doesn't matter, anyway. It worked out, didn't it? Let's find somewhere to sleep now," Kelovin said.

"Yes, I suppose it did," Miko relented.

Miko found a spot covered by large trees they could sleep under. Kelovin did not speak the rest of the night. The night was long. Kelovin couldn't get much rest. Every time he closed his eyes, he saw Pelmor's death, followed by a flashback to Ryga's death. In both cases, he had failed to do anything to save them. Ryga's death had been bad enough when he was literally unable to move. Pelmor's death was worse. He had taken a vow after

Ryga's death to get stronger so he could protect those around him. He had thought he'd been acquiring that strength the last few months. Pelmor's death was his rude awakening. He'd still been unable to do anything to save his friend. His depression deepened when he thought of how Pelmor had died because he was the one who needed saving. He had to get stronger.

At some point in the night, exhaustion finally took over. He drifted off to sleep. With it, came nightmares. He relived the death of his friend, accompanied by the imagined deaths of those he cared for back in Reshyr. In those nightmares, he was always helpless. There would be someone taking him to safety while others stood, and died, against whatever evil presented itself. He saw himself in Reyshyr, watching as Visrim burned through the Sleeping Trees. The pain of the trees and their occupants rang in his ears. Visrim was making his way toward Kelovin. Visrim's dark multicolored eyes locked on his own.

His mother rushed into Visrim's path to protect him. He yelled for her to get to safety, but she wouldn't move. Visrim smote her down with his fiery blade. The sight of his mother's death finally released Kelovin from the torment of the nightmare. Sweat plastered his body. He lay still, breathing heavily, while his mind sorted reality from nightmare. As calm came back over his body, Kelovin looked to his side to see Miko was already up eating some fruit.

"You didn't sleep very well last night," Miko commented.

Kelovin did not feel up to discussing the things on his mind, so he ignored Miko's comment. Instead, he asked, "Shall we get going? We still have a lot of ground to cover."

"Yeah, let's go," Miko said. Kelovin rose from the ground. He stared at the food set out for him. He didn't feel hungry, so he packed the food away along with everything else.

Miko seemed content to start their journey out in silence. Kelovin was grateful; he still wasn't in any mood to talk. He tried to escape the despair he felt by going through their plans to retrieve the god artifact. They were going to return to Eaglepoint so Miko could say goodbye to his friends there. From there, they would head to the uncharted lands Raizen had mentioned. It would probably take a while to find the location of the god artifact since everything they knew about it was only rumor.

He was so enveloped in reviewing their plan, he missed Miko tensing up and glancing around. Miko grabbed his arm to get his attention. "What is it?" Kelovin asked. They came to a stop.

"Whoever is there, come out. I can sense where you're hiding. If you don't reveal yourself, I will attack," Miko said.

"You killed my father. I've come to avenge his death," a green-haired elf with dark green eyes stepped out from his hiding spot. He looked to be Kelovin's age, perhaps slightly younger.

Kelovin's hand went straight to his blade. "How dare you talk of vengeance. You and all of your kind deserve to die," he said. He felt the fire magic pour into his body. He had not been taught yet how to properly use the magic. His use of it before happened instinctually out of desperation. The magic felt as though it was burning his insides, waiting for release. The feeling was invigorating. It made him feel powerful. He decided to manipulate the magic the same way he used his strength magic. He sent it coursing into his arm. His sword ignited. It was not what he'd envisioned happening, but he could make it work. The green-haired elf took a step backward. His eyes darted back and forth, scanning his surroundings.

Kelovin charged him. The boy took a couple of steps backward and stumbled. Sweat started dripping from his face. Kelovin did not slow. He aimed the flaming blade for the boy's neck. He knew one quick swing would be enough to sever the Elf's head from his body. A gust of wind blew his sword to the side in midswing. The extra momentum caused him to thrust his sword into the ground. The boy took the opportunity to get up and run away.

Kelovin spun to face Miko, "Why did you stop me?"

"He was only a young, confused boy. Killing him would have been wrong," Miko said.

"He's responsible for our capture and the death of Pelmor. He came here to kill us. He deserved whatever he got," Kelovin said.

"No. He was probably born in that place. The way he was raised can't be held against him. It was clear the boy was not ready for a real fight. Let it go," Miko said.

"Fine," Kelovin muttered. He looked at his sword. The impact into the ground, combined with the heat of his magical fire, had ruined it. His magic had destroyed yet another sword. Kelovin wrenched the sword out of the ground and chucked it as far as he could. He ignored the concerned look on Miko's face and turned to continue on their path toward Eaglepoint.

"I know you're dealing with the loss of Pelmor and the influence of fire magic, but if you're not careful, your eyes are going to go dark. Once your eyes are dark, it's hard to go back," Miko said. Kelovin stopped.

"What do you mean 'the influence of fire magic'?" Kelovin asked, turning back around.

"I told you before, each magic is attached to certain emotions. Usually, the emotion bleeds into the person involuntarily. Most adults don't have a problem with it because they've been getting used to it since birth. Your powers have been dormant your entire life, so the emotion is affecting you as it would a child still learning his powers," Miko said.

"So, you're saying I'm only pissed off because I have fire magic?" Kelovin asked, crossing his arms.

"No, I'm saying the side effects of your fire magic is making it worse and affecting your judgment," Miko said.

Kelovin processed what Miko was saying. It was uncharacteristic of him to act so rashly, even if he was grieving. "How am I supposed to know if what I'm doing is because of the extra emotion being thrown into my system? I wasn't able to tell the difference up to this point," Kelovin asked. The idea of doing something he would later regret frightened him. There was still so much he needed to learn about his origins. It would have been much easier to learn and deal with when he lived in Reshyr.

"Well, most people take years and years to get good at having control over their particular emotion. Many never master it. So, you'll have to grin and bear it for now," Miko said.

"I don't need this crap right now. I'm already dealing with more than I want to," Kelovin yelled, looking up into the sky. He wasn't talking to anyone in particular.

"Well, we should go so we can make it back to Eaglepoint tonight," Miko said. They set off at a walking pace. Neither of them offered more conversation during their travel.

The city came into view hours later. Miko led the way back to Burgor's house. Before they went in, Miko said, "We can stay the night here. We'll leave in the morning. If the girl asks where Pelmor is, please tell some lie. I don't want her to worry about the possibility of me dying while I'm away."

"All right," Kelovin said. The hours of secluded thought had helped him reign in the burning anger he felt within. It wasn't easy. Even insignificant things made him want to lash out at whatever was around him.

Miko opened the door and walked into the house with Kelovin behind him. Burgor rose to his feet, saying, "Here you are, my friend. I was starting to think you weren't ever going to return to Crow's Nest. I should have known you wouldn't be bested by a bunch of wizards." Burgor's voice boomed through the whole house.

"Are you kidding? No one can best my wits. I'll die an old man many years from now, not at the hands of amateurs," Miko said. Burgor and Miko looked at each other and laughed. Burgor walked over to Miko so he could wrap him up in a bear hug. He said in a soft voice, "I'm glad you're safe."

"I wouldn't be if it hadn't been for Kelovin," Miko said.

"Then I owe you my gratitude as well," Burgor told Kelovin. Kelovin didn't respond. Instead, he went to a corner of the house and sat against it.

"He is grieving the loss of his friend," Miko said in a quiet voice.

"Understandable," Burgor said. He turned to Kelovin again to say, "I'm terribly sorry for your loss. I understand how you feel. I lost my wife long ago." Kelovin gave him a slight nod to show he had heard him. He did not want to be drawn into conversation.

"Miko, you're back," the high voice of Burgor's daughter called out from the next room. She appeared in the doorway. Her eyes sparkled.

"You're darn right I'm back, Ella. I had to come see you again, didn't I?" Miko said. Ella ran to Miko. He swooped her up into his arms.

"Did you bring me something?" Ella asked, feeling around his clothes.

"Are you kidding? Would I ever leave you without bringing you back something? You'd have my head if I did. I like my head where it's at," Miko said.

"What is it?" Ella asked. Her eyes got wide.

Miko reached down to his boot. He pulled a flower from it. The petals unraveled from the smashed position they were in. Slowly, the flower returned back to look as if it had never been disturbed. The petals were vibrant, changing to different colors continuously.

"It's beautiful," Ella whispered.

"It only grows in the Traveling Forest. It can only grow on magic, but it can live through most anything," Miko said. Kelovin didn't remember seeing him take any flower of the sort while they were within the Traveling Forest. He didn't remember seeing it, either. Ella stared at the flower, watching it change from blue to red. Miko sat her on the ground. He put his hands on her shoulders, "Listen, I'm going to be leaving for a while. I don't know the next time I'll be back again, but I will be back." Burgor made a noise, shifting from one foot to the other.

"No," Ella yelled, throwing the flower to the ground. She grabbed his legs, sobbing into them. She spoke with her voice muffled by his pants, "You can't go. You belong here with me and daddy."

Miko pulled her off his legs, picked up the flower, and said, "I'm sorry. This is something I need to do. Don't worry, you know I'll be visiting again. I have to come back to give your flower more magic." He handed her the flower. She took it with trembling hands. "Now, go get something to put the flower in, then bring it back here," he said. Ella turned to go, still sniffling as she walked away.

"So, you're finally leaving Crow's Nest. I knew this day would eventually come. I wish it wasn't so soon," Burgor said.

"Don't worry, my friend. I'll be back like I said. Only to see your daughter, of course," Miko grinned.

"Makes sense," Burgor said, roaring with laughter. The girl walked back with the flower in a pot. She walked to Miko with the pot held out for him. Miko took it from her. Slowly, the flower rooted itself into the pot. It grew soft, green leaves.

"I fed it with a good dose of magic. It will be able to take care of itself for a while. Make sure you keep it safe," Miko said. He handed the pot back to her. When she took it, Miko smiled and caressed her cheek.

"Okay," Ella said, wiping her eyes. Seeing the bond between the two had a calming effect on Kelovin.

"Let's go, it's time to go back to sleep, little one," Burgor said. The two of them left the room. Burgor led Ella by the hand. Ella looked back at Miko with tears in her eyes until she was pulled out of sight.

"Ella loves you a lot," Kelovin said. He watched as Miko's cheerful expression was replaced by a saddened one. His bright yellow hair darkened, signifying the loss of his joy.

"It's mutual," Miko said. He lay down on the ground close to Kelovin.

"I didn't ever see a flower like the one you gave her in the forest," Kelovin said.

"It's rare, even in the Traveling Forest. We're starting early tomorrow. Get some sleep," Miko said.

Chapter Nine

It took them a couple of days to reach the uncharted lands. Much of their journey was passed in silence, except for training. Kelovin constantly threw himself into training his abilities. Miko helped him as much as he knew how. Since he spent every moment he wasn't walking on getting better, he was able to learn a lot but not nearly as much as he wanted to. Obtaining the power he needed was taking too long.

An enormous swamp marked the beginning of the uncharted lands. It was one of the reasons people had not done much exploring there. Kelovin's nose wrinkled at the swamp's stench. They were standing on soggy ground at the edge of the swamp. Murky water stretched out before them.

"Looks like they were right, after all," Miko said referring to the villagers fifteen minutes behind them. They had warned the Elves they would need a raft to cross the first part of the swamp to reach the village they sought. Kelovin carried it over his head. It was small and dinky-looking, but they were assured it would do its job. They were told that if they did not use it, they would sink into the soft mud below the water and drown.

Kelovin set the raft down on top of the water. "Why does it smell so bad?" Kelovin asked.

Miko shrugged his shoulders, "I don't know. Maybe there's a crazy amount of dead, rotting corpses under the water."

"Let's go," Kelovin said, ignoring Miko's answer. He was in no mood for his light-hearted jokes. Miko boarded the raft, carrying a large stick he found by the swamp's edge. There was barely enough room for the both of them on the raft. Kelovin was surprised it did not sink the second they stepped onto it. The villagers had also sold them a paddle to propel the raft across the swamp. Kelovin paddled their way across the water. Miko used his stick to take an experimental jab at the water. There was a momentary resistance about a foot down before it continued to sink. When Miko tried to pull it back, he found it was stuck. It slowly sank farther down.

"I guess you would drown," Miko laughed. "Better make sure you don't let us tip over. I wouldn't want to die a slow death."

"I have no intention of dying before I've had my revenge," Kelovin muttered angrily. Talk about death reminded him of Pelmor, no matter what the context was.

Miko saw Kelovin's red hair darken slightly. "You're bottling up a massive amount of rage. It's not good for you."

"You wouldn't understand," Kelovin growled.

Miko decided to change the subject, "I've been meaning to tell you more about our abilities. Since you've exhibited more than one power, you now have more than one color in your eyes and hair. You know the color of your eyes and hair is a dead giveaway of the type of power you have. However, there is a way to hide this information. As long as you're not currently using the branch of magic associated with a certain color, you can banish the color from your hair. You have to have one color present at all times, but you can control which one is showing. All you have to do is expel any traces of all other magic from your body."

"You only said hair. What about the eyes?" Kelovin asked.

"The eyes are a bit trickier. They like to retain their color. Most people try to hide their eyes when they're trying to be sneaky. The only way is if you don't summon a particular branch of magic for about six months, then the color will disappear from your eyes as well," Miko said.

Kelovin handed the paddle over to Miko. Miko accepted it. He continued rowing them across the swamp. Kelovin closed his eyes. He figured the fire magic should be the easiest to dispel from his body, as it was the most recent addition to his powers. He concentrated on telling his body to rid itself of all the fire magic lingering in his system. After a few minutes, he opened his eyes and asked, "Did it work?"

Miko chuckled, "No, not yet. Keep trying for a while." Miko paddled on without speaking while Kelovin continued practicing. The village turned out not to be far from the edge of the swamp. They'd only been traveling about an hour when it came into view. Had they been able to walk over dry land, they could have jogged there in about fifteen minutes. The village was settled on top of an island full of trees among the swamp's waters.

When their raft hit the edge, Miko carefully tested the ground with his foot. It appeared to be solid enough. He jumped onto the island. Besides a soft squelch, he did not sink into the ground. Once Kelovin saw Miko was safe, he joined him. The village wasn't much. There were only a dozen houses spread out on the land. None of the houses were well-made, either.

A broad, muscular man approached them, "Can I help you?"

"Yes, I have a question I think you might be able to answer," Miko said, "Why in the world would anyone want to live out here in the horrible, stinky swamp?"

The man barked with laughter, "We collect the slime weed growing here. Those plants are what smell so bad, but they're great for healing sick people. Only problem is, they're only found in the swamp. Unfortunate souls like myself get assigned to collect it."

"Unfortunate, indeed," Miko said.

"We're looking for one of the great artifacts of the gods," Kelovin said evenly.

The man looked at Kelovin with a frown, then turned back to Miko. "Your friend not pleasant."

"You'll have to excuse him, we've had some, uh, misfortunes," Miko explained. The man huffed but didn't say anything. Miko continued, "We are, however, looking for the artifact as my friend mentioned, and we're told the great masters of this village would be able to point us in the right direction."

The man roared with laughter, "I like you. You Elf with a tongue of gold. I will tell you what you seek, but first, we drink."

"We don't have time for drinking," Kelovin said.

"We drink!" the man roared louder.

Miko threw his arm around the man and bellowed, "We drink!"

The man threw his own arm around Miko, guiding him forward. He said loudly, "I knew you were a fine Elf."

Kelovin stomped after them. They paid him no attention. They came to a shack. The man threw the door open, revealing a storage area. It was completely stocked with liquor. "Wow, how did you come by all of this?" Miko asked.

"They like to make sure we stay happy, means they keep our liquor stores full," the man grinned broadly. He grabbed two mugs then hesitated, "Does Grumpy Elf want to drink?"

"No," Kelovin glared. "I'll wait." Kelovin went to a nearby tree and sat against it. He felt himself sink into the ground a little when he did.

"I didn't want Grumpy Elf to join anyway," the man said. He poured some brown liquid out of the barrel into their mugs then handed one to Miko.

Miko raised his mug into the air, "To new friends."

"New friends," the man agreed, tapping his mug against Miko's and immediately draining his cup. Miko followed suit. He drained his own cup almost as easily. "You're a good drinker, too, my friend. We shall see who can drink the most. My name is Kelm." Kelm filled their mugs once more.

Miko raised his mug again and said, "To good liquor." Kelm voiced his agreement by slapping his mug against Miko's and draining it once more. Miko did the same. Kelm filled them a third time.

This time, Kelm raised the mug and said, "Because we can." Miko hit his mug against Kelm's and they both drained them at the same time. After the fifth one, Kelm slowed down so he could sing songs. Most of them were crude songs about stealing virgins from their fathers, mixed with the occasional song about slaying monsters.

"So, about the artifact," Miko asked with a slur a couple of hours later.

"Tomorrow," Kelm said loudly. "It's not good to wander the swamp with so much liquor in you. Tonight, you sleep as my guest." Miko glanced over at Kelovin and saw he was sleeping.

"All right, then we'll sleep here tonight," Miko said.

"Follow me," Kelm led him to one of the makeshift houses. Inside there were two beds. There was barely any space for anything else. Kelm motioned to one bed then lay down on the other. Miko's head was spinning, so he gladly lay down. He passed out moments later.

The next morning, Miko woke up to Kelovin shaking his shoulder, "Miko it's time to go. Kelm is about to leave, you need to talk to him before he goes."

Miko groaned protest but sat up anyway. Then a smile appeared, "He refused to talk to you, eh."

Kelovin scowled, "Yes, but that isn't the point right now. The point is, if you don't catch him, we'll be stuck wandering around this swamp aimlessly because I'm not going to be stuck here another day."

"All right, I'm going," Miko said. Miko exited the house. He called out to Kelm, "Hey, Kelm, you mind helping out a friend before you go save the world one slime weed at a time?"

"I would love to, my friend," Kelm's voice boomed loudly. "Take your raft southwest till you hit ground. Then go on foot southwest for a few miles. There is a spot there where no one can travel. Anyone who tries ends up getting lost. Some never find their way back. It is a dangerous place to visit. I advise you not to go, but you are strong, I'm sure you be fine."

"Thank you, my friend. I'm sure we shall see each other again," Miko called back.

"I sure hope not," Kelovin muttered.

"He hasn't done anything to you, Kelovin," Miko said in a more serious tone than Kelovin had ever heard before.

"I don't care," Kelovin said, moving to retrieve their raft. Miko opened his mouth to make a response then closed it again. He followed after Kelovin. They did not have to go far before they hit land. The land was able to support them, although their feet still sunk into the mud a few inches. There were many spots where there were pools of water covering the ground. They both avoided those spots without having to say anything.

"I'm not sure we're going the right way," Miko said after they had been walking for two hours. "Kelm said it was only a few miles away."

"No, I think we're fine. He probably made it sound closer than it is," Kelovin said.

"I think we should turn around and look for the village again," Miko said.

"You only think so because you want to drink with Kelm again," Kelovin snapped.

"You know that's not why," Miko said.

"No, I don't. You seemed pretty happy doing it yesterday," Kelovin kept walking. Miko sighed to himself. He thought to himself that something really needed to be done about Kelovin. He continued on behind him.

They were only walking for a few more minutes when Miko called out with panic in his voice, "Kelovin." Kelovin ignored him. He thought he was going to complain about being lost again.

"Kelovin, look," Miko yelled.

"We aren't turning back," Kelovin yelled. He turned around to confront Miko. Instead, he found himself staring at a nine-foot-tall monster. Kelovin's eyes were level with rows of teeth coming from the chest of the towering creature. Its mouth was a-foot-and–a-half long, running vertically from its stomach to its chest. Kelovin took a step backward. The thing slid forward on one of its two massive legs. There was slime oozing from pores all over its body. The creature had four long arms coming from its body and eight red eyes circling the top of its head. Kelovin knew the creature must be a Groucken. He was taught about them as a child. He had never seen one before now. He looked past it to see there were two more approaching Miko.

Kelovin reached out for his fire magic, but he could feel it was even weaker than it normally was. He figured it must be because of the damp environment. He shot it out in a jet at the creature anyway. The flames had no effect on the creature. Kelovin had no desire to fight the thing at close range, so he continued to back up. He saw Miko unzipping the sides of his clothes behind the other two Groucken. He'd never even known there were zippers in Miko's clothing. When they were all unzipped, his clothes became much baggier.

Miko leaped into the air, spreading out his arms and legs. The clothes became taut, catching the air Miko produced beneath him, allowing him to fly over the Groucken's head to where Kelovin stood. "Let's get out of here," Miko said.

"That was amazing. How come I never knew you could fly?" Kelovin asked.

"There's no time right now. We need to run," Miko said. He was right. Kelovin ran as fast as he could in the opposite direction of the pursuing Groucken. He glanced behind them. To his relief, the Groucken were moving far slower than they were. They kept running even after the Groucken disappeared behind them.

Kelovin saw a cave ahead of them. It looked out of place compared to the rest of the swampland. He stopped to say, "Miko, I think the cave might be what we've been looking for this whole time."

"If I was a hidden artifact, I think I might be in there," Miko agreed.

"Let's take a closer look," Kelovin said. They approached the cave, keeping an eye out for the Groucken. When they were fifty feet from the cave's entrance, a large rock golem jumped down in front of the cave from the top of it. The ground shuddered beneath its weight. The golem got into a fighting stance but didn't move from its spot.

“He seems like he’s protecting the cave’s entrance to me. Must be something important in there,” Miko said.

“How are we supposed to get in? It doesn’t look easy to move,” Kelovin said.

“I can distract it while you sneak past to see what’s inside,” Miko said. Kelovin looked at Miko for a moment. He wanted inside the cave, but he didn’t want to lose another friend doing something reckless.

“It sounds like a plan, but only if you promise you’ll fly out of here and leave me here if you get in danger,” Kelovin said.

“You don’t have to worry about me. I’m not going to be done in by a big pile of rocks. You get ready to run as soon as it swings at me,” Miko said. Miko was already running toward the golem before Kelovin could protest. When Miko was close enough, the golem swung its massive arm at him as Miko had predicted. Miko spread out his arms and legs using a gust of wind to propel himself backward. He simultaneously used a large gust of wind to propel the golem’s swing faster. The golem lost its balance. Its fist smashed into the ground, bringing the golem to its knees.

Kelovin took the opportunity to run behind it into the cave. It was dark, but he was still able to see easily. It was one of the things he was grateful was the same between himself and the Elvin kind he grew up with. The cave became a large cavern after a few steps. He looked behind him and saw the golem was not pursuing.

He walked forward, looking around the cave. He was halfway through the cavern when his body froze in mid-step. He tried to move. He found he could not. A voice rang out, "I should kill you right now." An Elf with gray hair and eyes stepped into his view. He looked to be in his old age, yet his body did not show the weakness that usually accompanies age.

Kelovin realized his body was encased in magic. The magic felt odd, yet familiar at the same time. He focused his own strength magic on cutting through the bindings. His foot finished going to the ground, but then he was stuck again. The magic re-encased him.

The gray elf smiled, "Wow. I have not seen that technique used in centuries. I assure you, it will not work again. I am far more powerful than yourself."

Kelovin found he could still talk, so he said, "I hate people like you."

"What do you mean 'like me,' " the Elf asked.

"People who prey on others weaker than themselves for the fun of it. I will destroy all of you," Kelovin said.

"My, aren't we the angry one? You're jumping to conclusions. I do not seek to harm others. In fact, you shouldn't have even been able to make it this far. Someone helped you get in here. Whoever they are, I should like to have a talk with them. It would take far greater magic than yours to tear down the protective barrier I had out there."

"Who are you?" Kelovin asked.

"Dram," the Elf said. He studied Kelovin quietly for a moment, "I do find your story somewhat interesting. On your current path, I'm afraid your future is not long."

"How could you possibly know that?" Kelovin asked.

"I have my ways. I also know you came here seeking a 'god artifact,' as you call them. You will not find any here."

Kelovin stared at Dram, trying to figure out who he was and how he knew so much. It was obvious he was powerful. "Can you help me find the artifact?" Kelovin asked. "I must become stronger."

"Why?" Dram asked him.

"So I can kill those responsible for killing my friends and make sure people who treat others as their playthings never exist anymore," Kelovin said.

"It's not a good reason. I'm inclined to help you anyway. It could prove interesting. You're the one who is supposed to stop the world from ending, after all. I will not help you find this artifact. It's useless to you. Your path lies elsewhere. The first thing you must do is let go of your grief and hatred. It is a poison inside of you," Dram said.

"How can I stop hating the people who stole my best friend from me?" Kelovin yelled.

"You've bottled up your grief for your friend. You must let it out," Dram told him.

"I can't," Kelovin whispered weakly. "There isn't any time."

Dram laughed, "Time is an easy thing to produce." Dram closed his eyes for a moment. Kelovin felt a strange tugging sensation. Then his stomach felt like it had been tied into knots. "Sorry," Dram said. "Traveling to the past the first time can be uncomfortable."

"What do you mean, 'traveling to the past'?" Kelovin asked, trying to narrow his eyebrows, and finding he still couldn't move.

"I've taken us five months into the past to give us time, as you requested," Dram said. There was something about the way Dram said it– with such confidence. It made him believe they truly had traveled to the past.

Hope glimmered in him for a moment, "We must go back to Reshyr and stop me, Pelmor, and Ryga from ever leaving the city."

"We can't mess with the past. What is done is done. Even if we were to try to stop them, your friends would die anyway," Dram said. "You must deal with the passing of your friend."

Tears came to Kelovin's eyes. "I can't," he whispered.
"You will."

Defra Elf Powers

Color	Power	Emotion
Red	Fire	Anger
Yellow	Air	Joy/carefree
Blue	Water	Sadness
Green	Vegetation	Peace
Brown	Earth	Pride
Orange	Beast	Happy
Gold	Strength	Fear
Silver	Inanimate objects	Outward Clarity
Purple	Mind	in control
Pink	Seduction	Lust
White	Life	Charity/pure love
Black	Death	Hate
Gray	Time/space	Inward Clarity

www.ingramcontent.com/pod-product-compliance
Lightning Source LLC
Chambersburg PA
CBHW061156170626
46809CB00003B/1128

* 9 7 8 0 9 9 7 6 6 9 0 2 2 *